The Jewish Book of
1 ENOCH

WITH ILLUSTRATIONS

Translated by George Henry Schodde
Foreword by Eli Lizorkin-Eyzenberg

ISBN: 9781706201076

Table of Contents

Foreword

We invite you to embark on an exciting journey of discovery by reading this reprint of the First Book of Enoch. The text of this edition is an English translation by the late George H. Schodde updated and edited by us.[1] It is accompanied by the imaginative illustrations of a talented Colombian artist, Lyda Estrada. We've titled this edition, "The *Jewish* Book of 1 Enoch" to stress the obvious (but often overlooked) fact. Though Christians preserved the manuscripts from which this translation originates, Enoch is an excellent example of Jewish spiritual literature from the Second Temple era.[2] It preserves a worldview held by some Jews at the dawn of the new millennium. Many people are not familiar with extra-biblical books such as Enoch, but they shed light on so many important Jewish beliefs and traditions prevalent before the emergence of Christianity. Exposure to such ancient worldviews allows modern readers of the Bible to develop a better, more well-rounded understanding of ancient writings.

The interpretations of some biblical passages found in Enoch may have influenced the New Testament writers. First Enoch is quoted and alluded to by the New Testament authors multiple times. They simply assume its authenticity by reflecting on its material.[3] This book of

---

[1] George H. Schodde, The Book of Enoch: Translated from Ethiopic with Introduction and Notes (W. F. Draper, 1882).

[2] E. Isaac, "A New Translation and Introduction," in The Old Testament Pseudepigrapha, vol. 1 (New York; London: Yale University Press, 1983), 5.

[3] Robert Henry Charles, ed., Pseudepigrapha of the Old Testament, vol. 2 (Oxford: Clarendon Press, 1913), 163.

Enoch was viewed as spiritual and deemed useful by notable figures of early Christian history such as Irenaeus and Tertullian. Even so, Enoch's writings were never included in any major Christian canon and were never identified as Scripture by the majority of Christian believers.

The entire book can be easily read in a single evening. If you are a serious student of ancient texts, we suggest that you start by reading the entire work from beginning to end, in one sitting. It will help you appreciate the grand picture. Then get your pen, highlighter, or e-reader annotation device ready and make notes as you re-read it. We guarantee that many new ideas and perspectives will jump out at you from this text.

Once you have read the work a couple of times, take time to also read what other scholars have written about the Book of Enoch. We've provided a suggested reading list for further study (see the table of contents). This will help you understand the strong argument that the New Testament authors accepted some (or perhaps many) of the ideas presented in the Jewish Book of Enoch and allowed them to inform their theological perspectives.

Should Enoch be a part of the Holy Scripture? Was it a mistake to exclude this book from the Christian canon (as some Eastern Orthodox Christians have argued)? No. Pinchas and I are both quite happy with our Bibles just the way they are. There are many more Jewish literary works out there and they deserve our study but in the framework of extra-biblical material. Having said that, it is clear that this book is essential for understanding some key concepts that influenced the minds, and especially the cosmology, of ancient Jews. Before you delve into this extra-biblical text, take the time to review some key facts about this fascinating ancient document.

Book of Enoch or Books of Enoch?

There exists an entire collection of Enoch literature which in more recent days was arranged into three different books attributed to the biblical Enoch. They are, for various reasons, termed by scholars as 1st Enoch surviving in Ethiopian, 2nd Enoch surviving in Slavonic and some sections in Greek, and 3rd Enoch surviving in Hebrew. The "1st Enoch" is a collection of various apocalyptic visions experienced by a seer named Enoch. The "2nd Enoch" reworks, in a completely different style, the fifth chapter of Genesis and expands on the biblical stories of Enoch and Noah. The "3rd Enoch" (sometimes called "the Book of Palaces") is also quite different. It is a first-person account of Rabbi Ishmael as he allegedly ascends the heavenly realm and visits six heavenly palaces. There Rabbi Ishmael encounters an angel-like figure of Metatron. It is important to know that when early Christian authors quote (or mention) the Book of Enoch, they generally refer only to 1st Enoch. The other books from the Enoch collections came into existence later. This is why the text we provide for your study in this brief volume is 1st Enoch. The subsequent books from the Enoch collection are also relevant, but you should begin with this material first.

A Real Enoch?

Although these texts may claim to be written by Enoch, they are clearly not the work of a single author and certainly were not composed by the "Enoch" whom we know from the book of Genesis. The Enochian corpus is the product of multiple authors and later editors. Multiple people contributed to what is now known as The Book of Enoch.[4] The scholarly community assigns the first two books of Enoch to an era between the third century BCE and the first century CE with some portions dating slightly later.[5] The Hebrew book of Enoch (3rd Enoch) is considered to be even later composition.[6]

The material in the Books of Enoch does not reflect the deep antiquity to which the biblical Enoch belonged. No doubt you recall that in the Bible, Enoch is the son of Jared and father of Methuselah (Gen 5). This places him far earlier than the time period to which the Book of

---

[4] F. L. Cross and Elizabeth A. Livingstone, eds., *The Oxford Dictionary of the Christian Church* (Oxford; New York: Oxford University Press, 2005), 551.
[5] George W. E. Nickelsburg, "Enoch, First Book of," ed. David Noel Freedman, *The Anchor Yale Bible Dictionary* (New York: Doubleday, 1992), 508.
[6] P. Alexander, "A New Translation and Introduction," in *The Old Testament Pseudepigrapha*, vol. 1 (New York; London: Yale University Press, 1983), 223.

Enoch can reasonably be dated. The Book of Enoch clearly reflects interests, issues, concerns, languages, scripts, etc. of a much later era.

The Book of Enoch is an example of extra-biblical (pseudepigraphic) Jewish material. This means that it was written by an individual or group other than the person to whom it was formally attributed. In the ancient world, it was a common practice to attribute a literary composition to some significant historical character. In fact, there exist numerous ancient books "falsely" attributed to biblical characters including Abraham, Moses, Solomon, Elijah, Thomas, and Mary. Regardless of the formal attribution, we know for a fact that the claimed authors did not compose these books. In today's world, this sounds like trickery, but in the ancient world, this was an accepted practice. By ascribing a text to someone famous, the work both gained authority and honored the person in whose name it was written. The writer (or writers) believed the dreams, visions, and events described in the text to be the sort of things that would have been experienced by the Biblical character mentioned.

The ancients were no fools. They did not expect that their attributions would be taken literally. We, of course, must never judge the ancient world by our modern standards (even when those modern standards may be better). There is a wonderful Russian proverb "Со своим уставом в чужой монастырь не ходят" which can be roughly translated "No one goes to another monastery with his own set of rules". In the same way, we must first discover the practices and standards of the ancients (good or bad from our modern standpoint) and only then seek to understand those writings in their own original context. The Jewish book of Enoch affords such an opportunity.

Basic Outline of 1St Enoch

"The Watchers" (Chapters 1–36)

This section describes the corruption of man, the fallen angels, and God's final judgment. Chapters 1–5 are an introduction, claiming that the book is the blessing of Enoch, which is passed on to all the righteous. Chapters 6–36 describe angelic beings, speak of seven archangels, and focus on the fallen angels who are called the "sons of

God" (as in Gen 6). They are "the watchers" (literally "the awake ones"), rebellious angels who corrupted humans through fornication and magic. Enoch intercedes for these watchers, also called the Nephilim (literally "the fallen ones"), but to no avail.

"The Parables" (Chapters 37–71)

Chapters 37-71 speaks of angels and judgment. The parables of Enoch quote heavenly prayers, offer various words of wisdom, describe the interactions of angels and humans, and recount visions of paradise. This section also describes the Son of Man, a Messiah figure, particularly relevant as a New Testament background.

"The Palaces" (Chapters 72–82)

This section discusses the sun, moon, stars, and solar calendar. Enoch warns Methuselah that mankind will eventually corrupt the calendar. In the last days, the entire order of times will be disrupted and the "heavenly luminaries" themselves will be affected by this corruption.

"The Dreams" (Chapters 83–90)

In this section, Enoch relates several dreams, including a vision of the flood that would destroy the world. He retells the history of the world from the days of Adam to the final judgment in allegorical fashion. This section is sometimes called the *"Animal Apocalypse"* because (just as in Daniel and Revelation) various animals represent key people: Israelites, their oppressors, leaders of Israel, and even the Messiah himself.

"The Letter" (Chapters 92–105)

Similar to a concept of a "last will and testament," this section highlights the blessings of the righteous and the woes of sinners. The righteous are encouraged to persevere before the judgment comes. Enoch predicts ten weeks in which wickedness and evil will thrive on the earth, but in the end, the righteousness with prevail.[7]

---

[7] For the structure and content of this short summary we are greatly indebted to an article by Jonathan Alan Hiehle and Kelly A. Whitcomb, "Enoch, First Book of," ed.

Now that you know the basic facts about the 1ˢᵗ Book of Enoch, we invite you to enjoy this ancient Jewish book, to start exploring what many ancient Jews believed about the powers, people, and events relevant to the holy books that we love and revere.

Pinchas Shir
Eli Lizorkin-Eyzenberg

John D. Barry et al., *The Lexham Bible Dictionary* (Bellingham, WA: Lexham Press, 2016).

The Jewish Book of
1 ENOCH

The Watchers

CHAPTER 1
1. The words of the blessing of Enoch through which he blessed the chosen and just, who will exist on the day of tribulation when all the wicked and impious will be removed.
2. And then answered and spoke Enoch, a righteous man, whose eyes were opened by God so that he saw a holy vision in the heavens, which the angels showed to me, and from them I heard everything, and I knew what I saw, but not for this generation, but for the far-off generations which are to come.
3. Concerning the chosen I spoke and conversed concerning them with the Holy and Great One, who will come from his abode, the God of the world.
4. And from there he will step on to Mount Sinai, and appear with his hosts, and appear in the strength of his power from heaven.
5. And all will fear, and the watchers will tremble, and great fear and terror will seize them to the ends of the earth.
6. And the exalted mountains will be shaken, and the high hills will be lowered and will melt like wax before the flame.
7. And the earth will be submerged, and everything that is on the earth will be destroyed, and there will be a judgment upon everything, and upon all the just.
8. But to the just he will give peace, and will protect the

chosen, and mercy will abide with them, and they will all be God's and will be prosperous and blessed, and the light of God will shine for them.

9. And behold, he comes with myriads of the holy to pass judgment upon them, and will destroy the impious, and will call to account all flesh for everything the sinners and the impious have done and committed against him.

CHAPTER 2

1. I observed everything that took place in the heavens, how the luminaries, which are in the heavens, do not depart from their paths, that each one rises and sets in order, each in its time, and they do not depart from their laws.

2. See the earth and observe the things that are done on it, from the first to the last, how no work of God is irregular in appearing.

3. See the summer and the winter, how then the whole earth is full of water, and clouds and dew and rain rest over it.

CHAPTER 3.

1. I observed and saw how then all the trees appeared as if withered, and all their leaves are shaken off, except fourteen trees, whose leaves are not shaken off, but which abide with the old from two to three years, till the new come.

CHAPTER 4.

1. And again I observed the days of summer, how the sun is then above it [i.e. the earth], opposite to it, but you seek cool and shady places on account of the heat of the sun, and the earth also burns with fervent heat, but you cannot step on the earth or on a rock because of their heat.

CHAPTER 5

1. I observed how the trees cover themselves with the green of the leaves and bear fruit, but observe you all this and learn how he who lives forever has made all these for you;

2. how his works are before him in every year that comes, and all his works serve him and are not changed, but as God has ordained, so everything takes place.

3. And see how the seas and the rivers together accomplish their work.

4. But you have not persevered and have not done the commandment of the Lord, but have transgressed, and have slandered his greatness with

high and hard words from your unclean mouths. You hard-hearted, you will have no peace.

5. And therefore you will curse your days, and the years of your lives perish; the everlasting curse will increase and you will receive no mercy.

6. On that day you will give away your peace for an everlasting curse to all the just, and they will ever curse you as sinners, you together with the sinners.

7. but for the chosen, there will be light and joy and peace, and they will inherit the earth, but for you, the impious, there will be a curse.

8. And then also wisdom will be given to the chosen, and they will all live and not continue to sin; neither through wickedness nor through pride; but they in whom there is wisdom will be humble without continuing to sin.

9. And they will not be punished all the days of their lives, and will not die through plagues or judgments of wrath, but the number of the days of their lives will be completed, and their lives will become old in peace, and the years of their joy will be many in everlasting happiness and peace, for all the days of their lives.

CHAPTER 6

1. And it came to pass after the children of men had increased in those days, beautiful and comely daughters were born to them.

2. And the angels, the sons of the heavens, saw and lusted after them, and said one to another: "Behold, we will choose for ourselves wives from among the children of men, and will beget for ourselves children."

3. And Semjâzâ, who was their leader, said to them: "I fear that perhaps you will not be willing to do this deed, and I alone will suffer for this great sin."

4. Then all answered him and said: "We all will swear an oath, and bind ourselves mutually by a curse, that we will not give up this plan, but will make this plan a deed."

5. Then they all swore together and bound themselves mutually by a curse, and together they were two hundred.

6. And they descended on Ardîs, which is the summit of Mount Hermon; and they called it Mount Hermon because they had sworn on it and bound themselves mutually by a curse.

7. And these are the names of their leaders: Semjâzâ, who was their leader, Urâkibarâmêêl, Akibêêl, Tâmiêl, Râmuêl, Dânêl, Ezêqêêl, Sarâqujâl, Asâêl, Armers, Batraal, Anânî, Zaqêbê, Samsâvêêl, Sartaêl, Turêl, Jomjâêl, Arâzjâl. 8. These are the leaders of the two hundred angels, and the others all were with them.

CHAPTER 7
1. And they took unto themselves wives, and each chose for himself one, and they began to visit them, and mixed with them, and taught them charms and conjurations, and made them acquainted with the cutting of roots and of woods.
2. And they became pregnant and brought forth great giants whose stature was three you and ells.
3. These devoured all the acquisitions of mankind until men were unable to sustain themselves.
4. And the giants turned themselves against mankind in order to devour them.
5. And they began to sin against the birds and the beasts, and against the creeping things, and the fish, and devoured their flesh among themselves, and drank the blood thereof.

6. Then the earth complained of the unjust ones.

CHAPTER 8
1. And Azâzêl taught mankind to make swords and knives and shields and coats of mail, and taught them to see what was behind them, and their works of art: bracelets and ornaments, and the use of rouge, and the beautifying of the eye-brows, and the dearest and choicest stones and all coloring substances and the metals of the earth.
2. And there was great wickedness and much fornication, and they sinned, and all their ways were corrupt.
3. Amêzârâk taught all the conjurers and root-cutters, Armârôs the loosening of conjurations, Baraq'âl the astrologers, Kôkâbêl the signs, and Temêl taught astrology, and Asrâdêl taught the course of the moon.
4. And in the destruction of mankind, they cried aloud, and their voices reached heaven.

CHAPTER 9
1. Then Michael and Gabriel and Surjân and Urjân looked down from heaven and saw the great amount of blood which had been spilled on the earth,

and all the wickedness which had been committed over the earth.

2. And they said to one another: "The emptied earth re-echoes the sound of their [i.e. mankind's] cries up to the gates of heaven.

3. And now to you, O you holy ones of heaven, cry the souls of men, saying: 'Secure us judgment before the Most High.'

4. And they spoke to their Lord, to the King: 'O Lord of lords, God of gods, King of kings, the throne of your majesty is among all the generations of the world, and your name, holy and glorious, among all the generations of the world. You art blessed and praised!

5. You have made all things and all power is with you, all things are open before you and uncovered, and you see all things and nothing can hide from you.

6. See then what Azâzêl has done, how he has taught all wickedness on earth and has revealed the secrets of the world which were prepared in the heavens.

7. And Semjâzâ to whom you have given the power to be chief of his associates has made known conjurations.

8. And they have gone together to the daughters of men and have slept with them, with those women, and have defiled themselves, and have revealed to them these sins.

9. And the women have brought forth giants, and thereby the whole earth has been filled with blood and wickedness.

10. And now, behold, the souls which have died cry and lament to the gates of heaven, and their groans ascend, and they are not able to escape from the wickedness which is committed on the earth.

11. And you know everything before it comes to pass, and you know this and their circumstances, and yet you do not speak to us. What will we do in regard to this?"

CHAPTER 10

1. Then the Most High, the Great and Holy One, spoke and sent Arsjalâljûr to the son of Lamech, and said to him:

2. "Tell him in my name: 'Hide yourself!' and reveal to him the end which is to come. For the whole earth will be destroyed, and the water of the deluge is about to come over the whole earth, and what is upon it will be destroyed.

3. And now instruct him that he may escape and his seed remain on the whole earth."

4. And again the Lord spoke to Rufael: "Bind Azâzêl hand and foot, and put him in the darkness; make an opening in the desert, which is in Dudâêl, and put him there.

5. And lay upon him rough and pointed rocks, and cover him with the darkness that he may remain there forever, and cover his face that he may not see the light!

6. And on the great day of judgment, he will be cast into the fire.

7. And heal the earth which the angels have defiled, and announce the healing of the earth that I will heal it, and that not all the sons of men will be destroyed through the mystery of all the things which the watchers have spoken and have taught their sons.

8. And the whole earth was defiled through the example of the deeds of Azâzêl; to him ascribe all the sins."

9. And God said to Gabriel: "Go against the bastards and those cast off and against the children of fornication, and destroy the children of fornication and the children of the watchers from among men; lead them out, and let them loose that they may destroy each other by murder; for their days will not be long.

10. And they will all supplicate you, but their fathers will secure nothing for them, although they expect an everlasting life, and that each one of them will live five hundred years."

11. And God said to Michael: "Announce to Semjâzâ and to the others who are with him, who have bound themselves to women, to be destroyed with them in all their contamination.

12. When all their sons will have slain one another, and they will have seen the destruction of their beloved ones, bind them under the hills of the earth for seventy generations, till the day of their judgment and of their end, till the last judgment has been passed for all eternity.

13. And in those days they will be led to the abyss of fire, in torture and in prison they will be locked for all eternity,

14. And then he will burn, and be destroyed; they will be burned together from now on to the end of all generations.

15. And destroy all souls of lust and the children of the watchers, because they have oppressed mankind.

16. Destroy all oppression from the face of the earth, and all wicked deeds will cease, and the plant of justice and righteousness will appear, and deeds will become a blessing: justice and righteousness will be planted in joy forever.

17. Then all the just will bend the knee, and they will remain alive till they bring forth a thousand children, and they will complete all the days of their youth and their sabbath in peace.

18. And in those days the whole earth will be worked in justice, and will all be planted with trees, and will be full of blessings.

19. And all the trees of desire will be planted on it, and vines will be planted on it; the vine planted on it will bear fruit in abundance. And of all the seed sown on it one measure will bear ten thousand, and one measure of olives will make ten presses of oil.

20. And cleanse you the earth of all oppression and all injustice and all sin and all wickedness and all uncleanness which are produced on the earth: eradicate them from the earth.

21. And all the children of men will become just, and all the nations will worship me as God, and bless and all will worship me.

22. And the earth will be cleansed of all corruption and all sin and all punishment and all torment, and I will never again send a flood upon it, from generation to generation, to eternity."

CHAPTER 11

1. "And in those days I will open the store-rooms of blessings which are in heaven, in order to bring them down upon the earth, upon the deeds and labor of the children of men.

2. Peace and rectitude will become associates in all the days of the world, and in all the generations of the world."

CHAPTER 12

1. And previous to all these things Enoch was hidden, and not one of the children of men knew where he was hidden, and where he was, and what had become of him.

2. And all his deeds were with the holy ones and with the watchers in his days.

3. And I, Enoch, was praising the great Lord and the King of the world, and, behold, the watchers called to me, Enoch, the scribe, and said to me:

4. "Enoch, you scribe of justice, go, announce to the watchers of heaven, who have left the high heaven and the holy, eternal place, and have contaminated themselves with women, and have done as the children of men do, and have taken to themselves wives, and are contaminated in great contamination upon the earth.
5. But upon earth they will have no peace, nor forgiveness of sin; for they will not enjoy their children.
6. They will see the murder of their beloved ones, and they will lament over the destruction of their children and will petition to eternity, but mercy and peace will not be unto them."

CHAPTER 13
1. And Enoch, departing, said to Azâzêl: "You will have no peace; a great condemnation has come upon you, and he [i.e. Rufael, cf. 10:4] will bind you;
2. And alleviation and intercession and mercy will not be unto you, because you have taught oppression, and because of all the deeds of abuse, oppression, and sin which you showed to the children of men."
3. And then going, I spoke to them all together; and they were all afraid, fear and trembling seized them.
4. And they asked me to write a memorial petition for them that they thereby might attain forgiveness, and to carry their memorial petition before God into heaven.
5. For they could not, from now on, speak with him, nor could they raise their eyes towards heaven from shame on account of their sins for which they were being punished.
6. Then I wrote this memorial petition and prayed with reference to their souls and for each of their deeds, and for that which they had asked of me, that they thereby might obtain forgiveness and patience.
7. And going I sat down near the waters of Dan in Dan, which is to the right [i.e. south] of the evening side [i.e. west] of Hermon, and read their memorial petition till I fell asleep.
8. And, behold, a dream came to me, and visions fell upon me, and I saw the vision of chastisement to show to the sons of heaven, and to upbraid them.
9. And having become awake I went to them, and they were all sitting assembled lamenting at Ublesjâêl, which is between the

Lebanon and Sênêsêr, with their faces covered.

10. And I related before them all the visions that I had seen in my sleep and commenced to speak those words of justice and to upbraid the watchmen of heaven.

CHAPTER 14

1. This writing is the word of justice and the admonition of the watchers, who are from eternity, as the Holy and Great One commanded it in this vision.

2. I saw in my sleep what I now will relate with a tongue of flesh and with my breath, which the Great One has given to the mouth of men that they might converse with it and understand it in their hearts.

3. As he has created and given to men the power to understand the word of knowledge, thus also he has created me and given to me the power to upbraid the watchers, the sons of heaven.

4. "I have written your petition, and in my vision it appeared to me thus, that your petition will not be granted in all the days of the world, and that judgment has been passed over you, and nothing will be granted unto you.

5. And from now on you will not ascend into heaven to all eternity, and upon the earth, it has been decreed, they will bind you for all the days of the world.

6. But before this, you will have seen the destruction of your beloved children, and you will not be able to possess them, but they will fall before you by the sword.

7. Your petition for them will not be granted unto you, nor the one for yourselves; and while you are weeping and praying you cannot speak a single word from the writing which I have written."

8. And the vision appeared to me thus: behold, clouds in the vision invited me and a fog invited me; and the course of the stars and lightning drove and pressed me, and the winds in the vision gave me wings and drove me.

9. And they lifted me up into heaven, and I went till I approached near a wall which was built of crystals and a tongue of fire surrounded it; and it began to cause me to fear.

10. And I went into the tongue of fire and approached near to a large house, which was built of crystals, and the walls of this house were like a floor inlaid

with crystals, and the groundwork was of crystals.

11. The ceiling was like the course of the stars and of the lightning, and Cherubim of fire were between them, and their heaven was water.

12. A flaming fire surrounded the walls, and its doors burned with fire.

13. And I went into this house, and it was hot like fire and cold like ice, and there was nothing pleasant and no life in it: fear covered me, and trembling seized me.

14. And as I was shaking and trembling, I fell down on my face and saw in a vision.

15. And behold, there was a second house, larger than the other, all whose doors stood open before me, and it was built with a tongue of fire.

16. And in all things, it excelled in grandeur and magnificence and size, so that I cannot describe to you its magnificence and its size.

17. Its floor was fire, and above it was lightning and the course of the stars, and its ceiling was also a flaming fire.

18. And I looked and saw therein a high throne; its appearance was like the hoar-frost, and its circuit like a shining sun and voices of the Cherubim.

19. And from under the great throne came streams of flaming fire, and it was impossible to look at it.

20. And he who is great in majesty sat thereon; his garment shone more brilliantly than the sun and was whiter than any hail.

21. None of the angels were able to enter, nor any flesh to look upon the form of the face of the Majestic and Honored One.

22. The fire of flaming fire was round him, and a great fire stood before him, and none of those who were around him could approach him; ten thousand times ten thousand were before him, but he required not any holy counsel.

23. And the holy ones who were near him did not leave day or night, nor did they depart from him.

24. And I had had so long a veil upon my face, and I trembled; and the Lord called me with his own voice and said to me: "Come here, Enoch, and to my holy word!"

25. And he made me get up and I went to the door, but I bent my face downwards.

CHAPTER 15

1. And he answered and spoke to me with his word: "Hear, and fear not, Enoch, you just man and scribe of justice, approach here, and hear my words.

2. And go, say to the watchers of heaven, who have sent you, that you should petition for them: 'You should petition for men, and not men for you.

3. Why have you left the high, holy, and everlasting heaven, and lain with women, and defiled yourselves with the daughters of men, and taken wives unto yourselves, and acted as the children of earth, and begotten giants as sons?

4. While you were spiritual, holy, having eternal life, you defiled yourselves with women, and with the blood of flesh have begotten children, and have lusted after the blood of men, and have produced flesh and blood as they produce who die and are destroyed.

5. Therefore I have given them wives that they might impregnate them and children be born by them, as it is done on earth.

6. You were formerly spiritual, living an eternal life without death to all the generations of the world.

7. Therefore I have not made for you any wives, for spiritual beings have their home in heaven.

8. And now the giants, who have been begotten from body and flesh, will be called evil spirits on earth, and their dwelling-places will be upon the earth.

9. Evil spirits proceed from their bodies; because they are created from above, their beginning and first basis being from the holy watchers, they will be evil spirits upon the earth and will be called evil spirits.

10. But the spirits of heaven have their dwelling-places in heaven, and the spirits of the earth, who were born on the earth, have their dwelling-places on earth.

1. And the spirits of the giants, who cast themselves upon the clouds, will be destroyed and fall, and will battle and cause destruction on the earth, and do evil; they will take no kind of food, nor will they become thirsty, and they will be invisible.

12. And these spirits will not (?) rise up against the children of men and against the women because they have proceeded

from them. In the days of murder and destruction.

CHAPTER 16
1. And of the death of the giants, when the spirits have proceeded from the bodies, their flesh will decay without judgment; thus they will be destroyed till that day when the great judgment over all the great world will be completed over the watchers and the impious.
2. And now to the watchers who have sent you that you should petition for them who were formerly in heaven say:
3. 'You have been in heaven, and though the secrets were not yet revealed to you, still you knew illegitimate mysteries, and these you have, in the hardness of your hearts, related to the women, and through these mysteries, women, and men increase wickedness over the earth.'
4. Tell them, therefore: 'You have no peace!'"

CHAPTER 17
1. And they took me to a place where there were images like a flaming fire, and when they wished they appeared like men.
2. And he led me to the place of the whirlwind, and on a hill, the point of whose summit reached to heaven.
3. And I saw shining places, and the thunder at the ends thereof; in the depths thereof a bow of fire, and arrows and their quiver, and a sword of fire, and all lightning.
4. And they took me to the so-called water of life, and to the fire of the west, which receives every setting of the sun.
5. And I came to a river of fire, whose fire flows like water, and is emptied into a great sea which is towards the west.
6. And I saw all the great rivers, and came to the great darkness, and went there where all flesh wanders.
7. And I saw the mountains of the black clouds of winter and the place where all the waters of the deep flow.
8. And I saw the mouths of all the rivers of the earth and the mouth of the deep.

CHAPTER 18
1. And I saw the repositories of all the winds, and I saw how he had ornamented all the creation and the foundations of the earth with them.
2. And I saw the corner-stone of the earth, and I saw the four winds which support the earth

and the firmament of the heavens.

3. And I saw how the winds expand the heights of the heavens, and they remained between heaven and earth, and they are pillars of heaven.

4. And I saw the winds which turn the heavens, which lead down the course of the sun and all the stars.

5. And I saw the winds upon the earth which carry the clouds, and I saw the paths of the angels; I saw at the end of the earth the firmament of the heavens above.

6. And I proceeded towards the south; and it burns day and night there where seven hills of precious stones are, three towards the east, three towards the south.

7. But of those towards the east, one of colored stone, one of pearls, and one of antimony; and those towards the south of red stone.

8. But the middle one reached up to heaven, like the throne of God, of alabaster, and the summit of the throne of sapphire.

9. And I saw a burning fire which was in all the hills.

10. And there I saw a place, beyond the great earth; there the waters collected.

11. And I saw a great abyss in the earth, with columns of heavenly fire; and I saw among them columns of heavenly fire, which fall. and are without number, either towards the height or towards the depth.

12. And over that abyss, I saw a place which had no firmament of heaven above it, and no foundation of earth beneath it, and no water above it, and no birds upon it; it was a void place.

13. And there I saw a terrible thing: seven stars, like great burning mountains and like spirits, that petitioned me.

14. The angel said: "This is the place of the consummation of heaven and earth; it is a prison for the stars of heaven, and for the host of heaven.

15. And the stars that roll over the fire are they who have transgressed the command of God before their rising, because they did not come forth in their time.

16. And he was enraged at them, and bound them till the time of the consummation of their sins in the year of the mystery."

CHAPTER 19

1. And Uriel said to me: "Here will stand the souls of those

angels who have united themselves with women, and having assumed many different forms, have contaminated mankind, and have led them astray so that they brought offerings to the demons as to gods, namely on the day when the great judgment, on which they will be judged, will be consummated.

2. And their women having led astray the angels of heaven, will be like their friends."

3. And I, Enoch, alone saw this vision, the ends of all; and no man has seen them as I have seen them.

CHAPTER 20

1. And these are the names of the holy angels who watch:

2. Uriel, one of the holy angels, the angel of thunder and of trembling;

3. Rufael, one of the holy angels, the angel of the spirits of men;

4. Raguel, one of the holy angels, who takes vengeance on the earth and the luminaries;

5. Michael, one of the holy angels, namely set over the best portion of men, over the people;

6. Saraqâel, one of the holy angels, who is over the spirits of the children of men who induce the spirits to sin;

7. Gabriel, one of the holy angels, who is over the serpents and over the Paradise and the Cherubim.

CHAPTER 21

1. And I went around to a place where not one thing took place.

2. And I saw there something terrible, no high heavens, no founded earth, but a void place, awful and terrible.

3. And there I saw seven stars of heaven, tied together to it, like great mountains, and flaming as if by fire.

4. At that time I said: "On account of what sin are these bound, and why have they been cast here?"

5. And then answered Uriel, one of the holy angels, who was with me, conducting me, and said to me: "Enoch, concerning what do you ask, and concerning what do you inquire, and ask and art anxious?

6. These are of the stars who have transgressed the command of God, the Highest, and are bound here till ten thousand worlds, the number of the days of their sins, will have been consummated."

7. And from there I went to another place which was still

more terrible than the former. And I saw a terrible thing: a great fire was there, which burned and flickered and appeared in sections; it was bounded by a complete abyss, great columns of fire were allowed to fall into it; its extent and size I could not see, and I was unable to see its origin.

8. At that time I said: "How terrible this place is, and painful to look at!"

9. At that time answered Uriel, one of the holy angels, who was with me; he answered and said to me: "Enoch, why such fear and terror in you concerning this terrible place and in the presence of this pain?" 10. And he said to me: "This is the prison of the angels, and here they are held to eternity."

CHAPTER 22

1. And from here I went to another place, and he showed me in the west a great and high mountain-chain and hard rocks and four beautiful places.

2. And beneath them, there were places deep and broad and entirely smooth, as smooth as if a thing were rolled, and deep and dark to look at.

3. And this time, Rufael, one of the holy angels, who was with me, answered and said to me:

"These beautiful places are intended for this, that upon them may be assembled the spirits, the souls of the dead; for they have been created, that here all the souls of the sons of men might be assembled.

4. These places have been made their dwellings till the day of their judgment, and to their fixed period; and this period is long, till the great judgment will come over them."

5. And I saw the spirits of the children of men who had died, and their voices reached up to heaven and lamented.

6. At that time I asked the angel Rufael, who was with me, and said to him: "Whose soul is that one whose voice thus reaches to heaven and laments?"

7. And he answered and said to me, saying: "That is the spirit that proceeded from Abel, whom his brother Cain slew; and it laments on his account till his seed be destroyed from the face of the earth and his seed disappear from among the seed of men."

8. And at that time I, therefore, asked concerning him, and concerning the judgment of all, and said: "Why is one separated from the other?"

9. And he answered and said to me: "These three apartments

are made in order to separate the souls of the dead. And thus are the souls of the just separated: there is a spring of water, above it, light.

10. And thus also is one such apartment made for the sinners when they die, and are buried in the earth, without a judgment having been passed upon them during their lives.

11. Here their souls are separated in this great affliction until the great day of judgment and punishment and affliction upon the revilers to eternity, and the vengeance for their souls, and here he binds them to eternity.

12. And if it was before eternity, then this apartment has been made for the souls of those who lament and those who reveal their destruction when they were killed in the days of the sinners.

13. And thus it has been created for the souls of men who were not just, but sinners, who were complete in their crimes; and they will be with criminals like themselves; but their souls will not be killed on the day of judgment and will not be taken from here."

14. At that time I blessed the Lord of glory, and said: "Blessed is my Lord, the Lord of glory and of justice, who rules all things to eternity!"

CHAPTER 23

1. And from there I went to another place towards the west, to the ends of the earth.

2. And I saw a flaming fire which ran without resting, and did not cease from its course day or night, but continued regularly.

3. And I asked saying: "What is that which has no rest?"

4. At that time answered Raguel, one of the holy angels, who was with me, and said to me: "That burning fire which you sees running towards the west is the fire of all the luminaries of heaven."

CHAPTER 24

1. And from there I went to another place of the earth, and he showed me a mountain-chain of fire which flamed day and night.

2. And I went towards it and saw seven magnificent mountains, each one different from the other, and magnificent and beautiful rocks, everything magnificent and fine in appearance and of beautiful surface; three towards the east, one founded upon the other, and three towards the south,

one founded upon the other, and ravines, deep and winding, not one joining with the other. 3. And the seventh hill was between these; and in their heights they were all like the seats of a throne and surrounded with fragrant trees. 4. And among them was a tree such as I had never smelt before, neither among these nor among others; nor was there a fragrance like its; its leaves and buds and wood do not wither in eternity; its fruit is beautiful, like the fruit of the vine and the palm-tree. 5. And at that time I said: "Behold, this is a beautiful tree and beautiful to look at, and its leaves are fair, and its fruit very pleasant to the eye." 6. At that time answered Michael, one of the holy and honored angels, who was with me, who was over them [i.e. the trees].

CHAPTER 25
1. And he said to me: "Enoch, what do you ask me concerning, the fragrance of this tree and do seek to know?" 2. Then I, Enoch, answered him, saying: "Concerning all things I desire to know, but especially concerning this tree."

3. And he answered me, saying: "This high mountain which you have seen, whose summit is like the throne of God, is the throne where the holy and great God of glory, the Eternal King, will sit when he will descend to visit the earth with goodness, 4. And this tree of beautiful fragrance cannot be touched by any flesh until the time of the great judgment; when all things will be atoned for and consummated for eternity, this will be given to the just and humble. 5. From its fruits life will be given to the chosen; it will be planted towards the north, in a holy place, towards the house of the Lord, the Eternal King. 6. Then they will rejoice greatly, and be glad in the Holy One; they will let its fragrance enter their members, and live a long life upon the earth, as your fathers lived; and in their days no sorrow or sickness or trouble or affliction will touch them." 7. Then I blessed the Lord of glory, the Eternal King, because he had prepared such for the just men, and had created such, and said he would give it to them.

CHAPTER 26

1. And from here I went to the middle of the earth, and saw a place, blessed and fruitful, where there were branches which rooted in and sprouted out of a tree that was cut.

2. And here I saw a holy mountain, and beneath the mountain, towards the east, water which flowed towards the south.

3. And I saw towards the east another mountain of the same height, and between them a deep valley, but not broad: therein also water flowed along the mountain.

4. And towards the west of this was another mountain, lower than the former, not high, and below, between them, a valley; and other deep and sterile valleys were at the end of the three.

5. And all the valleys were deep and not broad, of hard rock. And trees were planted upon them. 6. And I was astonished on account of the rocks, and was astonished on account of the valley, and was very much astonished.

CHAPTER 27

1. Then I said: "For what purpose is this blessed land, which is entirely filled with trees, and this cursed valley between them?"

2. Then answered Uriel, one of the holy angels, who was with me, and said to me: "This cursed valley is for those who will be cursed to eternity, and here will be assembled all those who have spoken with their mouths unseemly words against God, and speak insolently of his glory, here they will be assembled, and here will be their judgment.

3. And in the latter days there will be the spectacle of a just judgment upon them in the presence of the just, in eternity forever; for this reason they who have found mercy will bless the Lord of glory, the Eternal King.

4. And in the days of their judgment they will bless him for his mercy, according to which he has assigned to them their lot."

5. Then I blessed the Lord of glory, and spoke to him, and remembered his greatness, as it is fitting.

CHAPTER 28

1. And from here I went towards the east, into the midst of the mountains of the desert, and saw only a plain.

2. But it was filled with trees of this seed, and water dropped down over it from above.

3. It was seen that the water which it sucked up was strong, as towards the north, so towards the west, and as in all places, so water and dew also ascended from here.

CHAPTER 29

1. And I went to another place, away from the desert, approaching the east of the mountains.

2. And there I saw trees of judgment, especially those that emitted the fragrance of frankincense and myrrh, and they were not like ordinary trees.

CHAPTER 30

1. And above, over these, over the eastern mountain, not far off, I saw another place, valleys with water that does not dry up.

2. And I saw a beautiful tree, and its fragrance was like that of a mastic.

3. And along the edges of these valleys, I saw fragrant cinnamon. And I advanced over these towards the east.

CHAPTER 31

1. And I saw another mountain in which were trees from which

water flowed, and it flowed like nectar, which is called Sarira and Galbanum.

2. And over this mountain, I saw another mountain, on which were aloe trees; and these trees were full of hard substance like almonds.

3. And in taking that fruit it was better than all the odors.

CHAPTER 32

1. And after these odors, as I looked towards the north, over the mountains, I saw seven mountains full of pleasant nard and fragrant trees and cinnamon and pepper.

2. And from here I went over the summits of those mountains, far towards the east, and passed far above the Erythraean sea, and went far from it and passed over the angel Zutêl.

3. And I came into the garden of justice, and I saw the mingled diversity of those trees; many and large trees are planted there, of attractive beauty and large and beautiful and magnificent, also the tree of wisdom; eating of it one learns great wisdom.

4. It is like the carob tree, and its fruit is like the grape, very good; the fragrance of this tree goes out and is spread far.

5. And I said: "This tree is beautiful; how beautiful and pleasant to look at!"

6. Then the holy angel Rufael, who was with me, answered and said to me: "This is the tree of wisdom from which your old father and your aged mother, who were before you, ate, and they learned wisdom, and their eyes were opened, and they learned that they were naked, and were driven out of the garden."

CHAPTER 33

1. And from here I went to the ends of the earth, and saw great animals there, and one differed from the other, and the birds differed as to their appearance, their beauty and voices, one differed from the other.

2. And to the east of these animals, I saw the ends of the earth, where the heavens rest and the portals of the heavens open.

3. And I saw where the stars come out from heaven, and I counted the portals out of which they come, and I wrote down all their outlets, each one, according to their number and their names, their connections and their positions and their times and their months, as the angel Uriel, who was with me, showed them to me.

4. He showed all things to me and wrote them down for me; also their names he wrote for me, and their laws and their deeds.

CHAPTER 34

1. And from here I went towards the north, to the ends of the earth, and there I saw a great and magnificent wonder, at the ends of the whole earth.

2. There I saw three portals of heaven open in the heavens; from each of them proceed north winds; when one of them blows, there is cold, hail, frost, snow, dew, and rain.

3. And out of one of the portals it blows for good; but when it blows from the two other portals, it blows with power, and there is misfortune upon the earth, and they blow with great power.

CHAPTER 35

1. And from here I went towards the west, to the ends of the earth, and saw there three open portals, as I had seen in the east, similar portals and similar outlets.

CHAPTER 36

1. And from here I went towards the south, to the ends of the earth, and there I saw three open portals of heaven; out of them come the south wind and dew and rain and wind.

2. And from here I went towards the east to the ends of the heavens, and there I saw the three portals of heaven open towards the east, and over them small portals.

3. Through each one of these small portals the stars of the heavens come and go every evening on the path which is shown to them.

4. And as I looked, I blessed, and thus each time I blessed the Lord of glory, who had made the great and glorious wonders, to show the greatness of his work to the angels and to the souls of men, that they might praise his work, and that all his creatures might see the works of his might, and praise the great work of his hand, and bless him to eternity.

The Parables

CHAPTER 37

1. The second vision of wisdom which Enoch, the son of Jared, the son of Mahalaleel, the son of Cainan, the son of Enos, the son of Seth, the son of Adam, saw.

2. And this is the beginning of the words of wisdom, which I commenced to speak and to relate to those who dwell on the earth: hear, ancestors, and see, descendants, the holy words which I will speak before the Lord of the spirits!

3. It is proper to name the former first, but from the descendants too we will not keep back the beginning of wisdom.

4. And up to the present time there was not given from before the Lord of the spirits the wisdom which I have received according to my knowledge, according to the pleasure of the Lord of the spirits, by whom the portion of life everlasting was given to me.

5. Three Parables were given to me; and I commenced to relate them to those who dwell on the earth.

CHAPTER 38

1. First Parable. When the congregation of the just will appear, and the sinners are condemned because of their sins, and expelled from the face of the earth,

2. and when the Just One will appear in the presence of the just who are chosen, whose deeds hang on the Lord of the spirits, and the light will appear to the just and to the chosen, who dwell on the earth,—where will be the habitation of the sinners, and where the resting-places of those who have denied

the Lord of the spirits? It were better had they not been born.
3. And when the secrets of the just will be revealed, then the sinners will be judged, and the impious will be expelled from the presence of the just and chosen.
4. And from that time those who hold the earth will not be powerful and exalted, nor will they be able to behold the face of the just, for the light of the Lord of the spirits is seen on the face of the holy and just and chosen.
5. And the mighty kings will perish at that time and will be given over into the hands of the just and holy. 6. And from that time on no one can ask for mercy from the Lord of the spirits, for their lives have ended.

CHAPTER 39.
1. And it will come to pass in these days that the chosen and holy children will descend from the high heavens, and their seed will become one with the children of men.
2. In those days Enoch received books of zeal and of anger, and books of disturbance and of expulsion, and "mercy will not be upon them," said the Lord of the spirits.

3. And at that time, a cloud and a whirlwind seized me from the face of the earth and carried me to the end of the heavens.
4. And here I saw another vision, the dwellings of the just and the resting-places of the holy.
5. Here my eyes saw their dwellings with the angels and their resting-places with the holy, and they asked and petitioned and prayed in behalf of the children of men, and justice like water flowed before them, and mercy like dew on the earth; thus it is among them to all eternity.
6. And in those days my eyes saw the place of the chosen of justice and of faith [fidelity], and how justice will be in their days, and the just and chosen without number before him to all eternity.
7. And I saw their dwelling under the wings of the Lord of the spirits, and all the just and chosen before him are ornamented as with the light of fire, and their mouths are full of blessings, and their lips praise the name of the Lord of the spirits, and justice before him will not cease.
8. Here I desired to dwell, and my soul longed for this place; here my portion has been

before, for such is established concerning me before the Lord of the spirits.

9. And in those days I blessed and exalted the name of the Lord of the spirits with blessings and praise, for he has strengthened me in blessing and praise according to the will of the Lord of the spirits.

10. For a long time, my eyes looked at this place, and I blessed him, saying: "Bless him, and let him be blessed from the beginning and to eternity!

11. Before him there is no ceasing; he knows, before the world was created, what the world is, and will be from generation to generation.

12. It is you whom they praise. those who do not sleep; they stand before your glory, and bless and glorify and exalt you, saying: 'Holy! Holy! Holy! the Lord of the spirits fills the earth with spirits.'"

13. And here my eyes saw all those who do not sleep, standing before him and blessing him, and they say: "Blessed art you, and blessed the name of the Lord to all eternity."

14. And my face was changed until I could see no more.

CHAPTER 40

1. And after that, I saw a thousand times thousand, and ten thousand times ten thousand beings, an innumerable and immense multitude, who stood before the glory of the Lord of the spirits.

2. I looked, and on the four sides of the Lord of the spirits I saw four faces, different from those standing, and I learned their names, which the angel who came with me announced as their names to me, and showed me all the secrets.

3. And I heard the voices of those four faces as they blessed before the Lord of glory.

4. The first voice blessed the Lord of the spirits to all eternity.

5. And I heard the second voice praising the Chosen One and the chosen ones, who hang on the Lord of the spirits.

6. And I heard the third voice asking and praying for those who dwell on the earth and petitioning in the name of the Lord of the spirits.

7. And I heard the fourth voice keeping off the adversaries, and not allowing them to come before the Lord of the spirits to accuse those who dwell on the earth.

8. After that, I asked the angel of peace who went with me,

who showed me all things that were hidden, and said to him: "Who are these four faces that I see, and whose voices I hear and have written them down?"
9. And he said to me: "The first is the holy Michael, merciful, slow to anger; and the second, who is over all sicknesses and over all the wounds of the children of men, is Rufael; and the third, who is over all the powers, is the holy Gabriel; and the fourth, who is over penitence and the hope of those who inherit everlasting life, if Fanuel."
10. And these are the four angels of God, the Most High, and the four voices I heard in those days.

CHAPTER 41
1. And after this, I saw all the secrets of heaven, and the kingdom as it is divided, and how the deeds of men are weighed upon scales.
2. There I saw the dwellings of the chosen, and the dwellings of the holy, and my eyes saw there how all the sinners were cast from there, they who had denied the name of the Lord of the spirits, and they are dragged away, and there is no rest for them because of the

punishments which proceed from the Lord of the spirits.
3. And there my eyes saw the secrets of the lightning and of the thunder, and the secrets of the winds, how they are divided to blow over the earth, and the secrets of the clouds and of the dew, and there I saw also from what place they proceed, and from from where they satisfy the dust of the earth.
4. And there I saw the closed repositories, and from them, the winds are divided out, and the repository of hail and the repository of fog and of the clouds; and his cloud hovers over the earth from the beginning of the world.
5. And I saw the repositories of the sun and of the moon, from where they come and to which they return, and their glorious return, and how one is more glorious than the other, and their fixed course, and how they do not leave their course, and how they add nothing to their course and take nothing from it, and preserve their fidelity one with the other, remaining steadfast in their oath.
6. And first the sun goes out, and makes his way according to the command of the Lord of the spirits, and strong is his name to all eternity;

7. and after this the hidden and the revealed course of the moon, completing the course of her way in that place by day and by night, one looking at the other [i.e. opposite each other] before the Lord of the spirits; and they give thanks and praise and do not rest, for their thanksgiving is rest for them.

8. For the shining sun makes many changes for a blessing and for a curse, and the course of the path of the moon is light to the just, and darkness to the sinners in the name of the Lord who created a separation between light and darkness, and divided the spirits of men, and strengthened the spirits of the just, in the name of his own justice.

9 For neither does an angel hinder, nor is any power able to hinder, for the Judge sees them all, and judges them all before him.

CHAPTER 42.

1. Wisdom did not find a place where she might live, and a dwelling-place was given to her in the heavens.

2. Wisdom came to dwell among the children of men, and found no dwelling-place; wisdom returned to her place and took her seat among the angels.

3. And injustice came forth from its repository; whom it did not seek, them it found, and dwelt with them, like the rain in the desert, and like dew in the thirsty land.

CHAPTER 43

1. And again I saw lightning, and the stars of heaven, and I saw how he called them all by their names, and they heard him.

2. And I saw that they were weighed on the scales of justice, according to their light, according to the width of their places, and the day of their appearance, and their course; one flash of lightning produces another, and their course according to the number of angels, and their fidelity they preserved among themselves.

3. And I asked the angel, who went with me, who showed me what was secret: "What are these?"

4. And he said to me: "The Lord of the spirits showed you a picture of them: these are the names of the just, who dwell on the earth and believe on the name of the Lord of the spirits to all eternity."

CHAPTER 44.

1. Also other things I saw in reference to the flashes of lightning; how they arise from the stars, and become lightning, and can leave nothing behind with them.

CHAPTER 45

1. And this is the second Parable concerning those who deny the name of the dwelling-place of the holy and of the Lord of the spirits.

2. They will not ascend to heaven, and will not come on the earth; such will be the portion of the sinners who deny the name of the Lord of the spirits, who are thus preserved to the day of suffering and sorrow.

3. On that day the chosen One will sit upon the throne of glory and will choose among their [i.e. men's] deeds and places without number, and their spirit will become strong in them when they see my Chosen One and those who have called upon my holy and glorious name.

4. And on that day I will cause my Chosen One to dwell among them and will transform heaven and make it a blessing and a light eternally.

5. And I will transform the earth and make it a blessing, and will cause my chosen ones to dwell thereon; and those who have committed sins and crimes will not step on it.

6. For I have seen and satisfied with peace my just ones, and have placed them before me; but for the sinners there awaits before me a judgment, that I may destroy them from the face of the earth.

CHAPTER 46

1. And there I saw one who had a head of days [i.e. was old], and his head was white like wool; and with him was a second whose countenance was like the appearance of a man, and his countenance was full of agreeableness, like one of the holy angels.

2. And I asked one of the angels, who went with me, and who showed me all the secrets, concerning this son of man, who he was and from where he was, and why he goes with the Head of Days?

3. And he answered and said to me: "This is the son of man, who has justice, and justice dwells with him, and all the hidden treasures he reveals, because the Lord of the spirits has chosen him, and his portion overcomes all things before the

Lord of the spirits in goodness to eternity.

4. And this son of man, whom you have seen, will arouse the kings and mighty from their couches, and the strong from their thrones, and will loosen the bonds of the strong, and will break the teeth of sinners.

5. And he will expel the kings from their thrones and from their kingdoms, because they do not exalt him and praise him, and do not acknowledge humbly why the kingdom was given to them.

6. And he will expel the countenance of the strong; and shame will fill them: darkness will be their dwelling-place and worms will become their couches, and they will have no hope of rising from their couches because they do not exalt the name of the Lord of spirits.

7. And these are they who master the stars of heaven, and raise their hands against the Most High, and tread the earth and live thereon, and all their doing is injustice and their doing manifests injustice, and their power is in their riches, and their faith is in gods which they have made with their hands, and they have denied the name of the Lord of the spirits.

8. And they will be cast out of the houses of his congregations, and of the faithful who hang on the name of the Lord of the spirits."

CHAPTER 47

1. And in those days the prayer of the just, and the blood of the just one ascend from the earth before the Lord of the spirits.

2. In these days the holy ones, who dwell in high heaven, will unite in one voice, and will petition and pray and praise and thank and bless the name of the Lord of the spirits, on account of the blood of the just which has been spilled, and the prayer of the just, that it may not be in vain before the Lord of the spirits, that judgment may be held over them, and they not suffer to eternity.

3. And in those days I saw the Head of days, as he sat upon the throne of his glory, and the books of the living were opened before him, and his whole host, which is in high heaven and around him, stood before him.

4. And the hearts of the holy ones were filled with joy, because the number of justice was fulfilled and the prayers of the just had been heard and the blood of the just one had been

demanded before the Lord of the spirits.

CHAPTER 48

1. And at that place, I saw an inexhaustible fountain of justice, and around it many fountains of wisdom and all the thirsty drank out of them and were filled with wisdom, and their dwelling-places were with the just and holy and chosen.
2. And at that hour that Son of man was called near the Lord of the spirits, and his name before the Head of days.
3. And before the sun and the signs were created, before the stars of heaven were made, his name was called before the Lord of the spirits.
4. He will be a staff to the just and the holy, upon which they will support themselves and not fall, and he will be the light of the nations, and he will be the hope of those who are sick in their hearts.
5. All who live upon the earth will fall down before him and bend the knee to him and will bless and praise him and will sing psalms to the name of the Lord of the spirits.
6. For this purpose, he was chosen and hidden before him before the world was created, and he will be before him to eternity.
7. And the wisdom of the Lord of the spirits has revealed him to the holy and the just, for he preserves the portion of the just, because they have hated and despised this world of injustice, and have hated all its deeds and ways in the name of the Lord of the spirits; for in his name they will be saved, and he will be the revenger of their lives.
8. And in those days the countenances of the kings of the earth, and of the mighty who possess the earth, will be bent down on account of the deeds of their hands, for on the day of their terror and trouble their souls will not be saved.
9. And I will put them into the hands of my chosen, like straw in fire and like lead in water; thus they will burn before the face of the just, and sink before the face of the holy, and no trace of them will be found.
10. And on the day of their trouble, there will be rest on the earth; before him, they will fall and not rise again, and there will be no one to take them with his hands and lift them up because they have denied the Lord of the spirits and his Anointed.

The name of the Lord of the spirits be blessed!

CHAPTER 49

1. For wisdom is poured out like water, and glory does not cease before him to all eternity.
2. For he is powerful in all the secrets of justice; and injustice, like a shadow, will end, having no stability, because the Chosen One has arisen before the Lord of the spirits and his glory is to all eternity, and his power to all generations.
3. In him dwells the spirit of wisdom, and the spirit of him who imparts understanding, and the spirit of doctrine and of power, and the spirit of those asleep in justice.
4. And he will judge the secrets, and no one will be able to speak a vain word before him, because he is the Chosen One before the Lord of the spirits, according to his will.

CHAPTER 50

1. And in those days there will be a change for the holy and chosen, and the light of the days will dwell over them, and glory and honor will be turned over to the holy.
2. And on the day of trouble, evil will gather over the sinners, but the just will overcome through the name of the Lord of the spirits; and he will show it to the others, that they may repent, and cease the work of their hands.
3. And they will have no honor before the Lord of the spirits, but in his name, they will be saved, and the Lord of the spirits will have mercy on them, for his mercy is great.
4. And he is just in his judgment, and before his glory, and injustice will not stand in his judgment: whosoever will not repent will be destroyed.
5. From now on I will not have mercy on them, says the Lord of the spirits.

CHAPTER 51

1. And in those days the earth will return that entrusted to it, and Sheol will return that entrusted to it, which it has received, and hell will return what it owes.
2. And he will choose the just and holy from among them, for the day has come that they be saved.
3. And the Chosen One in those days will sit upon his throne, and all the secrets of wisdom will proceed from the thoughts of his mouth, for the Lord of the spirits has given it to him and has honored him.

4. And in those days the mountains will skip like rams, and the hills spring like lambs satisfied with milk, and they will all be angels in heaven.

5. Their faces will shine in gladness, because the Chosen One has arisen in those days, and the earth will rejoice, and the just will live thereon, and the chosen will walk and move thereon.

CHAPTER 52

1. And after those days, at that place, where I had seen all the visions of that which is hidden—for I was taken up by the whirling of the wind and carried toward the west—

2. there my eyes saw the secrets of heaven, all things that will be on the earth, a mountain of iron, and a mountain of copper, and a mountain of silver, and a mountain of gold, and a mountain of soft metal, and a mountain of lead.

3. And I asked the angel who went with me, saying: "What are those things which I have seen in secret?"

4. And he said to me: "All these things which you have seen are for the power if his Anointed, that he may command and be powerful on the earth."

5. Then this angel of peace answered and said to me: "Wait for a little, and you will see, and there will be revealed to you every secret that the Lord of the spirits has planted.

6. These mountains which you have seen, the mountain of iron, and the mountain of copper, and the mountain of silver, and the mountain of gold, and the mountain of soft metal, and the mountain of lead, all these will be before the Chosen One like wax in the presence of fire, and like the water which falls down from above on these mountains, and will be weak before his feet.

7. And it will come to pass in those days that no one will save himself, not with gold and not with silver: no one will be able to save himself or to flee.

8. And there will be no iron for war and no clothing for a breast-plate; metal will not aid and zinc will not aid, and will not be beaten out, and lead will not be desired.

9. And all these things will disappear and be destroyed from the face of the earth when the Chosen One will appear before the face of the Lord of the spirits."

CHAPTER 53.

1. And there my eyes saw a deep valley, whose mouth was open, and all those who dwell upon the earth and sea and islands will bring him gifts and presents and tokens of submission, but that deep valley will not be filled.

2. And they commit crimes with their hands, and everything they make they devour criminally, they, the sinners; but they will be destroyed in the presence of the Lord of the spirits, they, the sinners, and will be chased from off the face of his earth continually to all eternity.

3. For I have seen the angels of punishment, going and preparing all the instruments for Satan.

4. And I asked the angel of peace who went with me: "These instruments, for whom have they been prepared?"

5. And he said to me: "These are prepared for the kings and the mighty of this earth that they be destroyed with them.

6. And after this the Just and Chosen One will cause the house of his congregation to appear; From now on it will not be hindered in the name of the Lord of the spirits.

7. And these mountains will be in his presence like the earth, and the hills will be like a fountain of water, and the just will rest from the oppression of the sinners."

CHAPTER 54

1. And I looked and turned toward another side of the earth, and I saw there a deep valley with a burning fire.

2. And they brought the kings and the powerful, and put them into the deep valley.

3. And there my eyes saw how they make instruments for them, iron chains of immense weight.

4. And I asked the angel of peace, who went with me, saying: "These chain instruments, for whom have they been prepared?"

5. And he said to me: "These have been prepared for the hosts of Azâzêl, to imprison them and put them into the lowest hell: and their jaws will be covered with rough stones, as the Lord of the spirits has commanded.

6. Michael and Gabriel, Rufael and Fanuel, they will overpower them on that great day, will throw them on that day into the oven of burning fire, that the Lord of the spirits may avenge himself on them on account of their injustice, because they

became subject to Satan, and have led astray those who dwell on the earth."

7. And in those days the punishment from the Lord of the spirits will come, and all the repositories of water, which are above in the heavens, and also the fountains of water, which are under the heavens, and which are under the earth, will be opened.

8. And all the waters will be joined with the waters which are above in the heavens, but the water which is in high heaven is the masculine, and the water which is beneath on the earth is the feminine.

9. And then will be destroyed all those who dwell on the earth and those who dwell under the ends of heaven.

10. And through this, they know their injustice, which they have done on the earth, and therefore they are destroyed.

CHAPTER 55

1. And after that the Head of Days repented and said: "In vain have I destroyed all who dwell on the earth."

2. And he swore by his great name: "From now on I will not act this way towards all those who dwell on the earth, and I will place a sign in the heavens; and it will be a token of fidelity between me and them to eternity, as long as heaven is above the earth.

3. And then it will be according to my command; when I desire to overpower them by the hand of the angel on the day of trouble and suffering, before this my anger and my punishment, my anger and my punishment will remain over them," says the Lord of the spirits.

4. "You mighty kings, who will dwell on the earth, you will be about to see my Chosen One, as he sits on the throne of my glory, and judges Azâzêl and all his associates, and all his hosts in the name of the Lord of the spirits."

CHAPTER 56

1. And I saw there the hosts of the angels of punishment walking and holding chains of iron and of metal.

2. And I asked the angel of peace, who went with me, saying: "To whom are these going, holding them [i.e. the chains]?"

3. And he said to me: "Each one to his chosen and his beloved, that they be thrown into the deep abyss of the valley.

4. And then that valley will be filled with their chosen and beloved, and the day of their lives will be ended, and the day of their error will, from that time on, not be counted."

5. And in those days the angels will assemble, and turn their heads toward the east, towards the people of Parthia and Media, in order to excite the kings, and that a spirit of disturbance come over them, and disturb them from off their thrones, that they come forth from their resting places like lions, and like hungry wolves amidst their flocks.

6. And they will ascend and step upon the land of their chosen, and the land of his chosen will be before them a threshing-floor and a path.

7. But the city of my just will be a hindrance to their horses, and they will take up a battle amongst themselves, and their right will become strong against themselves, and a man will not know his neighbor or his brother, nor the son his father or his mother, until there will be sufficient bodies by their death and their punishment over them,—it will not be in vain.

8. And in those days the mouth of Sheol will be opened, and they will sink into it; and their destruction, Sheol, will devour the sinners from the presence of the chosen.

CHAPTER 57
1. And it came to pass after this that I saw again a host of wagons, upon which men were riding, and they came upon the wind from the east and from the west to the south.

2. And the noise of their wagons was heard, and as this commotion took place, the holy ones from heaven noticed it; and the pillars of the earth were moved from their place, and it was heard from the ends of the earth to the ends of the heavens in ONE day.

3. And they will all fall down and bend the knee before the Lord of the spirits. And this is the end of the second Parable.

CHAPTER 58
1. And I began to speak the third Parable concerning the just and concerning the chosen.

2. Blessed are you, the just and chosen, for your portion is glorious!

3. And the just will be in the light of the sun, and the chosen in the light of everlasting life; and there will be no end to the days of their life, and the days

of the holy will be without number.

4. And they will seek the light and will find justice with the Lord of the spirits; there will be peace to the just with the Lord of the world.

5. And after that, it will be said to the holy, that they should seek in heaven the secrets of justice, the portion of faith [fidelity], for it has risen like the sun on the earth, and darkness has disappeared.

6. And there will be an unceasing light, and in the number of days, they will not enter, because darkness will be destroyed first, and the light will be mighty before the Lord of the spirits, and the light of rectitude will be strong in eternity before the Lord of the spirits.

CHAPTER 59

1. And in those days my eyes saw the secrets of the lightning, and the masses of light, and their judgments; and they flashed for a blessing and for a curse, as the Lord of the spirits desired.

2. And there I saw the secrets of the thunder, and how when it resounds above in the heavens its sound is heard; and they showed me the dwelling-places of the earth, and the thunder, either for peace or a blessing or for a curse, according to the word of the Lord of the spirits.

3. And after that, all the secrets of the luminaries and of the lightning were shown to me, as they flash for a blessing and for satisfaction.

CHAPTER 60

1. In the year five-hundred, and in the seventh month, on the fourteenth day of the month, of the life of Enoch. In that Parable, I saw that the heaven of heavens shook tremendously, and the host of the Most High, and the angels, a thousand times thousand, and ten thousand times ten thousand, were disturbed exceedingly.

2. And then I saw the Head of days sitting upon the throne of his glory, and the angels and the just ones stood around him.

3. And a great trembling took hold of me, and fear seized me; my loins were bent and were loosened, and my whole being melted together, and I fell down on my face.

4. And the holy Michael sent another holy angel, one of the holy angels, and he raised me up. And as he raised me my spirit returned, for I had not been able to endure the sight of

this host and of that trembling and shaking of heaven.

5. And the holy Michael said to me: "On account of what vision is such trembling? Up to to-day was the day of his mercy, and he was merciful and slow to anger over those who dwell on the earth.

6. But when the day and the power and the punishments and judgments come, which the Lord of the spirits has prepared for those who bow to the judgment of justice, and for those who deny the judgment of justice, and for those who take his name in vain—that day has been prepared a covenant for the chosen, and a test for the sinners.

7. And on that day two monsters will be distributed, a female monster, named Leviathan, to dwell in the depth of the sea, over the fountains of the waters.

8. But the masculine is named Behemoth, who occupies, with his breast, a void desert called Dêndâin, in the east of the garden where the chosen and holy will dwell, where my grandfather was taken up, the seventh from Adam, the first of men whom the Lord of the spirits made.

9. And I asked that other angel that he should show me the power of those monsters, how they were separated on ONE day, and that one descended into the depths of the sea and the other to the desert land.

10. And he said to me: "You son of man, you desire to know here that which is a secret."

11. Then the other angel, who went with me, spoke to me, and showed me that which was secret, the first and the last, what is in the heavens on high, and in the earth in the deep, and on the ends of the heavens, and on the foundations of heaven, and in the repositories of the winds;

12. And how the spirits are divided, and how weighing is done, and how the fountains and the winds are counted according to the power of the spirit, and the power of the lights of the moon, and that is it a power of justice, and the divisions of the stars according to their names, and how each division is divided;

13. and peals of thunder according to the places where they fall, and all the divisions that are made among the flashes of lightning that lightning may take place, and their hosts obey.

14. For the thunder has places of rest for the awaiting of its peal, and thunder and lightning are inseparable, and although not one, both go together through the spirit and are not separated.

15. For when the lightning flashes, the thunder utters its voice, and the spirit causes a rest during the flash, and divides equally between them, for the treasury of their flashes is like the sand; and each one of them, in its flash, is held with a bridle, and turned back by the power of the spirit, and is pushed forward, according to the number of the directions on the earth.

16. And the spirit of the sea is masculine and strong, and according to the strength of his power, he draws it [i.e. the sea] back with a bridle, and in like manner it is pushed forward, and scattered in all the mountains of the earth.

17. And the spirit of the hoar-frost is his own angel, and the spirit of hail is a good angel.

18. And he has left go the spirit of the snow on account of its strength, and it has a special spirit, and that which ascends from it is like smoke, and its name is frost.

19. And the spirit of the fog is not joined with them in their repositories, but it has a special repository, for its course is in clearness and in light and in darkness and in winter and in summer, and its repository is the light, and it [i.e. the spirit] is its angel.

20. And the spirit of the dew has its dwelling-place at the ends of the heaven and is connected with the repositories of the rain, and its course is in winter and in summer; and its clouds and the clouds of the fog are connected, and one gives to the other.

21. And when the spirit of rain moves out of its repository the angels come and open the repository, and lead it out, and when it is scattered over all the earth, and also as often as it is joined to the waters of the earth.

22. For the waters are for those who live on the earth; for they are the nourishment for the earth from the Most High, who is in heaven; therefore rain has its measure, and angels receive it.

23. All these things I saw towards the garden of the just.

24. And the angel of peace, who was with me, said to me: "These two monsters are prepared to be

fed, according to the greatness of God, that the punishments from God be not in vain, and sons will be killed with their mothers, and children with their fathers.

25. When the punishments from the Lord of the spirits will rest over them it will rest, so that the punishments from the Lord of the spirits may not come in vain over those; after that there will be a judgment in his mercy and his patience."

CHAPTER 61

1. And I saw in those days that long cords were given to those angels, and they took to themselves wings, and flew, and went towards the north.

2. And I asked the angel, saying: "Why have these taken the long cords, and have gone away?" And he said to me: "They went out to measure."

3. And the angel, who went with me, said to me: "These bring the measures of the just and the ropes of the just, that they may support themselves on the name of the Lord of the spirits to all eternity.

4. And the chosen will begin and dwell with the chosen, and these measures will be given to faith [fidelity], and will strengthen the word of justice.

5. And these measures will reveal all the secrets of the depths of the earth, and those who have been destroyed by the desert, and those who have been devoured by the fish of the sea, and by the beasts, that they return and support themselves on the day of the Chosen One, for none will be destroyed before the Lord of the spirits, and none can be destroyed.

6. And then received a command all who dwell in the heights of heaven, and ONE power, and ONE voice, and ONE light, like the fire, was given to them.

7. And that one first they blessed and exalted and glorified with wisdom, and showed themselves wise in speech and in the spirit of life.

8. And the Lord of the spirits placed his Chosen One on the throne of his glory, and he will judge all the deeds of the holy ones in heaven, and will weigh their deeds on scales.

9. And when he will raise his countenance to judge their paths that are secret by the word of the name of the Lord of the spirits, and their path in the way of the just judgment of the highest God, then they will all speak with ONE voice, and

bless, and praise, and exalt, and glorify the name of the Lord of the spirits.

10. And then will cry out all the host of the heavens, and all the holy ones above, and the host of God, Cherubim and Seraphim and Ophanim, and all the angels of power, and all the angels of supremacies, and the Chosen One, and the other powers on the earth, above the water, on that day;

11. And will raise ONE voice, and will bless, and glorify, and praise, and exalt, in the spirit of faith [fidelity], and in the spirit of wisdom and of patience, and in the spirit of mercy, and in the spirit of judgment and of peace, and in the spirit of goodness, and will all say with ONE voice; 'Blessed is he, and blessed be the name of the Lord of the spirits, in eternity, and to eternity.'

12. And all who do not sleep in high heavens will bless him; all his holy ones, who are in heaven, will bless him, and all the chosen, who dwell in the garden of life, and every spirit of light, who is able to bless, and glorify, and exalt, and say: 'Holy,' to your sacred name, and all flesh, which will exceedingly praise and bless your name to all eternity.

13. For great is the mercy of the Lord of the spirits, and he is slow to anger, and all his doing, and all his power, as much as he has made, he has revealed to the just and to the chosen, in the name of the Lord of the spirits.

CHAPTER 62

1. And thus the Lord commanded the kings and the powerful and the exalted and those who dwell on the earth, and said; "Open your eyes, and lift up your horns, if you are able to recognize the Chosen One."

2. And the Lord of the spirits sat on the throne of his glory, and the spirit of justice was poured out over him, and the word of his mouth slew all the sinners and all the impious, and they were destroyed before his face.

3. Then will stand up on that day all the kings and the powerful and the exalted and those who hold the earth, and will see him and will know that he sits on the throne of his glory, and that the just are judged in justice before him, and that there is no word spoken in vain before him.

4. And pain will come over them, like a woman who is in travail, and to whom the birth is

hard, when the son enters the mouth of the mother, and she has pain in giving birth.

5. And one portion of them will look upon the other and will tremble and cast down their countenances, and pain will seize them when they see this Son of the woman sitting on the throne of his glory.

6. And the powerful kings and all who hold the earth will honor, and bless, and exalt him who rules over all, who was hidden.

7. For formerly the son of man was hidden, and the Most High preserved him before his power and has revealed him to the chosen.

8. And the congregation of the holy and the chosen will be sown, and all the chosen will stand before him on that day.

9. And all the powerful kings and the exalted and they who rule the earth will fall before him upon their faces, and will worship and will hope in this Son of man, and will petition him and ask him for mercy.

10. And that Lord of the spirits will only press them, that they hasten to leave his presence and their countenances will be filled with shame, and darkness will be heaped upon their countenances.

11. And the angels of punishment will receive them to take vengeance on them because they have abused his children and his chosen.

12. And they will be a spectacle for the just and for his chosen; they will rejoice over them, because the wrath of the Lord of the spirits rests upon them, and the sword of the Lord of the spirits is drunk with them.

13. And the just and chosen will be saved on that day, and from that moment will not see the face of the sinners and of the unjust.

14. And the Lord of the spirits will dwell over them, and they will dwell with this son of man, and will eat and lie down and rise again with him to all eternity.

15. And the just and the chosen will have risen from the earth, and will have ceased to cast down their faces, and will be clothed with the garments of life.

16. And these will be the garments of life before the Lord of the spirits, and your garments will not become old, and your glory will not decrease before the Lord of the spirits.

CHAPTER 63

1. And in those days the powerful kings, who hold the earth, will petition the angels of punishment, to whom they are delivered, that they should give them a little rest, so that they could fall down and worship before the Lord of the spirits, and could acknowledge their sins before him.

2. And they will bless and glorify the Lord of the spirits, and will say: "Blessed is the Lord of the spirits, and the Lord of kings, the Lord of the powerful, and the Lord of the rulers, and the Lord of glory, and the Lord of wisdom, and every secret is clear.

3. And your power is to all generations, and your glory to all eternity: deep are your secrets all and without number, and your justice without reckoning.

4. Now we know that we should praise and bless the Lord of kings, and him who rules over all the kings."

5. And they will say: "Who will give us rest, that we might praise and thank and bless him, and be believers before his glory?

6. And now we long for a little rest, and do not find it; we are driven away, and do not receive it; the light has ceased before us,

and darkness is our dwelling-place to all eternity.

7. For before him we have not believed, and have not honored the name of the Lord of the kings, and we have not praised the Lord in all his doing, and our hope was in the scepter of our kingdom and in our glory.

8. And in the day of our trial and our trouble he did not save us, and we do not find rest to believe that our Lord is faithful in all his deeds and in all his judgments and his justice, and that his judgment does not respect persons.

9. And we will disappear before his face on account of our deeds, and all our sins are counted in justice."

10. Now they will say to them: "Our souls are satisfied with unjust goods, but it does not prevent our going to the flames of the pain of hell."

11. And after that their countenances will be filled with darkness and shame before that Son of man, and they will be expelled from his presence, and a sword will dwell in their midst before his countenance.

12. And thus said the Lord of the spirits: "This is the ordinance and judgment of the mighty and the kings and the exalted and those who hold the

earth before the Lord of the spirits."

CHAPTER 64
1. And I saw other faces in that place in secret.
2. I heard the voice of the angel saying: "These are the angels who descended from heaven upon the earth, and have revealed to the children of men that which was secret, and have led astray the sons of men that they committed sin."

CHAPTER 65
1. And in those days Noah saw the earth that it was curved and that its destruction was near.
2. And he lifted up his feet from there, and went to the ends of the earth, and called to his grandfather Enoch; and Noah said with a bitter voice: "Hear me! hear me! hear me!" three times.
3. And he said to him: "Tell me what is it that has been done on the earth, that the earth is so tired out and shaken? May I not be destroyed with it!"
4. And after this time there was a great trembling on the earth, and a voice was heard from heaven, and I fell on my face.
5. And Enoch, my grandfather, came and stood by me and said

to me: "Why do you so bitterly and lamentingly cry to me?
6. A command has come from before the presence of the Lord over all those who dwell on the earth, that their end is at hand, because they know all the secrets of the angels, and all the violence of the adversaries, and all the powers of secrecy, and all the powers of those who practice sorcery and the powers of fascination, and the powers of those who make metal images of the whole earth;
7. and also how silver is produced from the dust of the earth, and how soft metal originates on the earth.
8. For lead and zinc are not produced like the former; a fountain it is which produces them, and an angel who stands in it; and that angel is excellent."
9. And after that my grandfather Enoch took hold of me with his hand, and raised me up, and said to me: "Go, for I have asked the Lord of the spirits concerning this shaking of the earth.
10. And he said to me: 'On account of their injustice their judgment is completed; and will not be counted before me concerning the months which they have searched out, and through which they have

learned that the earth will be destroyed and those who live thereon.

11. And for them there will be no place of refuge to eternity, because they have showed them that which was secret, and they will be judged; but not you, my son; the Lord of the spirits knows that you are clean and free of this blame concerning the secrets.

12. And he has strengthened your name among the holy, and will preserve you from those who dwell on the earth, and will strengthen your seed in justice for kings and great honors; and from your seed will proceed the fountain of the just and the holy, without number, to eternity."

CHAPTER 66

1. And after that, he showed me the angels of punishment, who are prepared to come in order to open all the powers of the water which is under the earth, that it may be a judgment and destruction over all those who live and dwell on the earth.

2. And the Lord of spirits commanded the angels who went forth, that they should not lift up their hands, but should wait; for these angels are over the power of the waters.

3. And I went away from the presence of Enoch.

CHAPTER 67

1. And in those days the voice of God was with me, and he said to me: "Noah, behold your portion has ascended to me, a portion without blame, a portion of love and of goodness.

2. And now the angels are making a wooden building, and when they are gone to that work, I will lift up my hands upon it and will preserve it; and out of it will be [i.e. come] the seed of life, and a change will come so that the earth does not remain empty.

3. And I will strengthen your seed before me to all eternity and will scatter those who dwell with you over the face of the earth, and it [i.e. the seed] will be blessed and increased over the earth in the name of the Lord."

4. And they will enclose those angels who showed injustice in that flaming valley which my grandfather Enoch showed to me before, in the west, in the mountains of gold and of silver and of iron and of soft metal and of zinc.

5. And I saw that valley, in

which there was a great shaking and a shaking of the waters.

6. And as this took place there was produced from that flaming, flowing metal, and out of the shaking that shook them, at that place, an odor of sulphur, and it united with those waters; and that valley of the angels who had led astray burned under that earth.

7. And through the valley of that earth come rivers of fire, where those angels who had led astray those who dwell on the earth are condemned.

8. And those waters will be in those days for the kings and the powerful and exalted and those who dwell on the earth, a medicine of the soul and of the body, but for a judgement of the spirit, because their spirits are full of lust, that they be punished in their bodies, because they have denied the Lord of the spirits, and see their judgments daily, and still believe not in his name.

9. And as the burning of their bodies increases there will be a change in their spirit to all eternity; for no one will speak a vain word before the Lord of the spirits.

10. For the judgment comes over them, because they believe in the lust of their flesh, and deny the spirit of the Lord.

11. And those waters themselves, in those days, suffer a change, for when those angels will be condemned on those days, the heat of those fountains of the waters changes, and when the angels ascend, this water of the fountains changes and becomes cold.

12. And I heard the holy Michael answering and saying: "This judgment wherewith the angels are condemned is a testimony for the kings and the powerful and for those who hold the earth.

13. For these waters of judgment are a healing of the angels and a death to their bodies, but they will not see and will not believe that those waters change, and will become a fire, which burns to eternity."

CHAPTER 68
1. And after that my grandfather Enoch gave me the signs of all the secrets in a book, and the Parables which had been give to him, and he compiled them for me in the words of the book of the Parables.

2. And on that day the holy Michael answered, saying to Rufael: "The power of the spirit forces me and angers me, and

on account of the severity of the judgment of the secrets, the judgment over the angels; who can endure the severity of the judgment which is passed and remains, and before which they melt away?"

3. And the holy Michael answered again and said to Rufael: "Who is he whose heart is not softened concerning it, and whose reins are not shaken by this word? A judgment has come over them from [i.e. on account of] those whom they have led out."

4. And it came to pass as he stood before the Lord of the spirits, the holy Michael spoke to Rufael: "And I will not be for them under the eye of the Lord, for the Lord of the spirits is angered at them, because they act as if they were like gods.

5. Therefore judgment which is hidden comes over them, to all eternity; therefore, neither angel nor man will receive his portion, but they alone will receive their judgment to all eternity."

CHAPTER 69

1. And after this judgment, they will terrify and anger them, because they showed this to those who dwell on the earth.

2. And behold the names of those angels! and these are their names: the first of them is Semjâzâ, the second Arestîqîfâ, the third Armên, the fourth Kakabâêl, the fifth Turêl, the sixth, Rûmjâl, the seventh Dânêl, the eighth Nûqaêl, the ninth Barâqêl, the tenth Azâzêl, the eleventh Armers, the twelfth Batarjâl, the thirteenth Basasâêl, the fourteenth Anânêl, the fifteenth Turjâl, the sixteenth Simâpîsîêl, the seventeenth Jetarêl, the eighteenth Tûmâêl, the nineteenth Tarêl, the twentieth Rûmâêl, the twenty-first Izêzêêl.

3. And these are the heads of the angels, and the names of their chiefs over a hundred and the chiefs over fifty and the chiefs over ten.

4. The name of the first Jeqûn; he is the one who has led astray all the children of the holy angels, and has led them down on the earth, and has led them astray through the daughters of men.

5. And the second is called Asbeêl; he is the one who has taught the children of the holy angels the wicked device, and has led them astray to destroy their bodies with the daughters of men.

6. And the third is called Gâdreêl; he is the one who has taught the children of men all

the blows of death, and led astray Eve, and showed to the children of men the instruments of death, the coat-of-mail and the shield and the sword for battle, and all the instruments of death to the sons of men.

7. And from his hand, they have come over those who dwell on the earth, from that time to eternity,

8. And the fourth is called Pênêmû; he has taught the sons of men the bitter and the sweet and taught them all the secrets of their wisdom.

9. He taught men writing with ink and writing surfaces, and thereby many sinned from eternity and to eternity and up to this day.

10. For men were not born to the purpose that they should thus strengthen their fidelity with a quill and with ink.

11. For man was not created otherwise than the angels, that they should remain just and pure, and death, which destroys all things, would not have touched them, but through this their knowledge they are destroyed, and through this power it devours me.

12. And the fifth is named Kasdejâ; he has taught the sons of men all the wicked beatings of the spirits and the demons, the beatings of the birth in the womb, that it [i.e. the birth] fall, and the beatings of the soul, the bites of the serpent, and the beatings which take place at noon, the son of the serpent whose name is Tabâ't.

13. And this is the number of Kesbeêl, who showed the head of the oath to the holy ones, when he dwelt high in glory; and his name is Bêqâ.

14. And this one said to the holy Michael that he should show them the secret name, that they might see that secret name, and that they might mention this name in the oath, and they may tremble before that name and the oath, those that showed to the children of men all that is secret.

15. And this is the power of that oath, for it is powerful and strong, and he placed this oath Akâe' into the hands of the holy Michael.

16. And these are the secrets of this oath, and they were strengthened by his oath, and heaven was suspended before the earth was made, and to eternity.

17. And by it the earth was founded on the water, and from the secret places of the mountains come beautiful

waters for the living, from the creation of the world to eternity.
18. And by that oath, the sea was created, and as its foundation he placed for it sand for the time of rage, and it dare not pass over from the creation of the world and to eternity.
19. And by that oath, the depths were strengthened and stand and do not move from their places, from eternity and to eternity.
20. And by that oath, the sun and the moon complete their course and depart not from their commands from eternity and to eternity.
21. And by that oath, the stars complete their courses, and he calls their names and they answer him from eternity and to eternity.
22. And also the spirits of the water and of the winds, and of all the zephyrs and their paths, according to all the unions of the spirits.
23. And in it are preserved the repositories of the voice of thunder and of the light of the lightning, and there are preserved the repositories of hail and of the hoar-frost, and the repositories of the fog, and the repositories of the rain and of the dew.

24. And all these believe in and render thanks before the Lord of the spirits, and praise him with all their power, and their food is all thanksgiving, and they thank and praise and exalt in the name of the Lord of the spirits to all eternity.
25. And over them this oath is strong, and they are preserved by it, and their paths are preserved, and the courses are not destroyed.
26. And there was great joy among them, and they blessed and honored and exalted because the name of the Son of man had been revealed unto them.
27. And he sat upon the throne of his glory, and the sum of the judgment was given to him, the Son of man, and he causes to disappear and to be destroyed the sinners from the face of the earth, and also those who have led astray the earth.
28. They will be bound with chains and will be imprisoned in the assembling-place of destruction, and all their work will disappear from the face of the earth.
29. And from that time on there will be nothing that will be destroyed, for he, the Son of man, has appeared, and sits on the throne of his glory, and all

wickedness will disappear before his face and depart; but the word of that Son of man will be strong before the Lord of the spirits. This is the third Parable of Enoch.

CHAPTER 70

1. And it came to pass after this that his name was elevated during his lifetime to that Son of man, to the Lord of the spirits, away from those who dwell on the earth.
2. And it was elevated on the wagons of the spirit, and the name departed in their midst.
3. And from that day I was not drawn in their midst, and he set me between two winds, between the north and the west, there where the angels took the cords to measure for me the place for the chosen and for the just.
4. And there I saw the first fathers and the just, who dwell in this place from the beginning.

CHAPTER 71

1. And it came to pass after this that my spirit was hidden, and it ascended into the heavens; there I saw the sons of the angels stepping on a flame of fire; their clothes were white and also their garments, and the light of their faces was like crystal.
2. And I saw two rivers of fire, and the light of that fire flamed like hyacinth, and I fell on my face before the Lord of the spirits.
3. And Michael, an angel from among the chiefs of the angels, took me by the right hand and lifted me up, and led me out to all the secrets of mercy and to the secrets of justice.
4. And he showed me all the secrets of the ends of heaven, and all the repositories of the stars and of the luminaries, and why they proceed into the presence of the holy ones.
5. And the spirit moved Enoch into the heaven of heavens. And I saw there in the midst of the light how there was something which was built of crystal stone, and between these stones tongues of living fire.
6. And my spirit saw how a fire surrounded this house, on the four sides rivers full of living fire, and how they surrounded this house.
7. And around about were Seraphim and Cherubim and Ophanim; these are they who do not sleep, but guard the throne of his glory.
8. And I saw angels who could not be numbered, a thousand times thousand, and ten thousand times ten thousand

surrounded that house, and Michael and Rufael, Gabriel and Fanuel, and the holy angels who are in the high heavens enter and leave that house.

9. And Michael and Gabriel, Rufael and Fanuel, and many holy angels without number came out of that house;

10. And with them the Head of days, his head white and clean as wool, and his garments beyond description.

11. And I fell on my face, and all my flesh melted, and my spirit was changed; and I cried with a loud voice, with the spirit of power, and I blessed and honored and exalted.

12. And these blessings, which proceeded from my mouth, were pleasing before that Head of days.

13. And that Head of Days came with Michael and Gabriel, Rufael and Fanuel, and with thousands and with ten thousand times thousand angels without number.

14. And that angel came to me and greeted me with his voice and said to me: "You art a son of man who was born to justice, and justice dwells over you, and the justice of the Head of days will not depart from you."

15. And he said to me: "He calls 'Peace' unto you in the name of the world which is to come, for thence peace proceeds since the creation of the world, and thus it will be to you to eternity and from eternity to eternity.

16. And all who will continue to walk in your path (you, whom justice does not leave in eternity), their dwelling-places will be with you, and they will not be separated from you in eternity and from eternity to eternity.

17. And so long life will be with that Son of man, and peace will be to the just, and his right path to the just, in the name of the Lord of the spirits to all eternity.

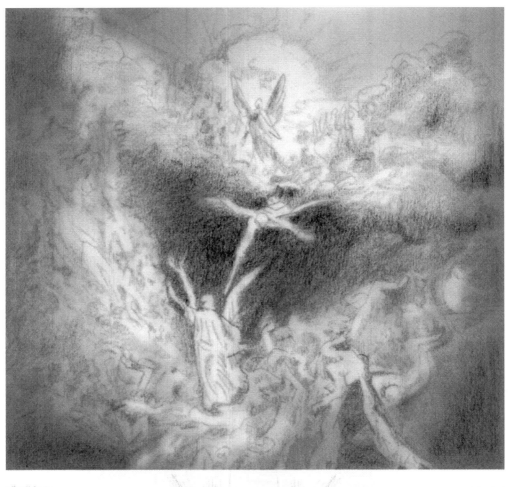

The Heavenly Luminaries

CHAPTER 72

1. The book of the courses of the luminaries of heaven, how it is with each one of them, as to their classes, their governments, and their times, as to their names and origin, and as to their months, which their leader Uriêl, a holy angel who was with me, showed to me, and their whole description as it is he showed to me, and how it is with respect to all the years of the world and to eternity, till a new creation is made which will continue to eternity.

2. And this is the first law of the luminaries: the luminary sun has its ascent in the portals of the heavens which are towards the east, and his descent in the western portals of heaven.

3. And I saw six portals, out of which the sun ascends, and six portals into which the sun descends; the moon also rises and sets in these portals, and the leaders of the stars and those led by them; six in the east and six in the west, and all, each after the other, aright; also many windows to the right and to the left of these portals.

4. And first comes forth the great luminary called the sun; and his circuit is like the circuit of the heavens, and he is entirely filled with flaming and heating fire.

5. The wagons on which he ascends are driven by the wind, and the sun descending disappears from the heavens and returns through the north in order to reach the east, and is led that he comes to that portal and shines on the surface of heaven.

6. And thus he comes forth, in the first month, in the great portal, and he comes forth from the fourth of these six portals towards the east.

7. And in that fourth portal, from which the sun comes forth in the first month, there are twelve window openings, from which a flame proceeds when they are opened in their time.

8. When the sun rises from the heavens he comes out of that fourth portal thirty mornings, and descends directly into the fourth western portal of heaven.

9. And in those days the day is daily lengthened, and the nights nightly shortened to the thirtieth morning.

10. And in that day the day is two parts longer than the night, and the day is exactly ten parts and the night eight parts.

11. And the sun comes forth from this fourth portal and sets in the fourth and returns to the fifth portal of the east thirty mornings, and comes forth from it and descends into the fifth portal.

12. From then on the day is lengthened two parts, and the day is eleven parts, and the night is shortened and is seven parts.

13. And the sun returns to the east and goes into the sixth portal, and comes forth and descends into the sixth portal, thirty-one mornings on account of its sign.

14. And on that day the day is longer than the night, and the day will be double the night, and the day is twelve parts, and the night is shorter and is six parts.

15. And the sun is raised so that the day is shortened and the night is lengthened, and the sun returns to the east and enters the sixth portal and rises from it and sets thirty mornings.

16. And when the thirty mornings are completed the day diminishes by exactly ONE part, and the day is eleven parts and the night seven parts.

17. And the sun comes forth from this sixth portal in the west and goes to the east and rises in the fifth portal thirty mornings and sets in the west again in the fifth portal.

18. On that day the day diminishes two parts, and the day will be ten parts and the night eight parts.

19. And the sun comes forth from that fifth portal and descends into the fifth portal of the west and rises in the fourth portal, on account of its sign, thirty-one mornings and descends in the west.

20. On that day the day is equal to the night and becomes equal, and the night is nine parts and the day nine parts.

21. And the sun comes forth from that portal and sets in the west and returns to the east and comes forth from the third portal thirty mornings and sets in the west in the third portal.

22. And on that day the night is longer than the day to the thirtieth morning, and the day becomes shorter daily to the thirtieth morning, and the night is exactly ten parts and the day eight parts.

23. And the sun comes forth from that third portal and sets in the third portal in the west and returns to the east, and the sun goes into the second portal of the east thirty mornings, and in like manner into the second portal in the west of the heavens.

24. And on that day the night is eleven parts and the day seven parts.

25. And the sun comes forth on that day from the second portal and descends in the west into the second portal and returns to the east in the first portal thirty-one mornings and descends into the west into the first portal.

26. And on that day the night will be so long that it will be the double of the day, and the night is exactly twelve parts and the day six parts.

27. And with that the sun has completed his stations, and he again returns to his station and enters in this portal thirty mornings; he rises and sets opposite it in the west.

28. And on that day the night diminishes in length by ONE part, and is eleven parts and the day seven parts.

29. And the sun returns and goes into the second portal of the east and returns to his course thirty mornings, rising and setting.

30. And on that day the night diminishes in length, and the night is ten parts and the day eight parts.

31. And on that day the sun comes forth from the second portal and descends in the west and returns to the east and rises in the third portal

thirty-one mornings and sets in the west of the heavens.

32. And on that day the night is shortened and is nine parts, and the day is nine parts, and the night is equal with the day, and the year has exactly three hundred and sixty-four days.

33. And the length of the day and of the night, and the shortness of the day and of the night—by the course of the sun they are made separated.

34. On that account, the day-course becomes longer daily and the night-course shorter nightly.

35. And this is the law and the course of the sun and his return when he returns; sixty times he returns and comes out, that is the great, eternal luminary which is called the sun to all eternity.

36. And that which thus ascends is the great luminary, as it is called on account of its appearance, according to the command of the Lord.

37. And thus he ascends and descends, and is not diminished, and does not rest, but runs day and night in his chariot, and his light shines seven times stronger than that of the moon; but as regards size they are both equal.

CHAPTER 73

1. And after this law, I saw another law with reference to the smaller luminary whose name is moon.

2. And her circuit is like the circuit of the heavens, and her chariot in which she rides is driven by the wind, and in a measure, light is given to her.

3. Every month her ascent and her descent is changed; her days are like the days of the sun, and when her light is equal [full] her light is the seventh part of the light of the sun.

4. And thus she rises. And her beginning in the east comes forth on the thirtieth morning, and on that day she becomes visible and is for you the beginning of the moon, on the thirtieth morning, together with the sun in the portal where the sun proceeds.

5. And the one half is prominent by the seventh part, and her whole circuit is empty, and there is no light with the exception of the one seventh part of the fourteen parts of light.

6. And on that day when she takes up the seventh part and the half of her light, her light contains one seventh and one

seventh part and the half of it. She sets with the sun.

7. And when the sun rises the moon also rises with him and takes a half portion of light, and in that night in the beginning of her morning on her first day the moon sets with the sun, and is darkened in that night, with the seventh and the seventh portions and the half of one.

8. And she will rise on that day with exactly the seventh part, and will come out and become smaller from the rising of the sun and shine the rest of her days, with the seventh and the seventh part.

CHAPTER 74

1. And I saw another course and law for her, making her monthly course according to that law.

2. And Uriel, the holy angel, who is the leader of them all, showed me all things, and I wrote down all their positions as he showed them to me, and I wrote down their months as they were and the appearance of their lights till fifteen days are completed.

3. And in seven single parts she completes all her light in the east, and in seven single parts she completes all her darkness in the west.

4. And in certain months she changes her settings, and in certain months she goes her peculiar course.

5. And in two the moon sets with the sun, in those two portals which are in the middle, in the third and in the fourth portal.

6. She comes forth seven days, and turns and returns again by that portal through which the sun comes; and in that she completes all her light and recedes from the sun; and enters in eight days into the sixth portal, through which the sun comes forth.

7. And when the sun comes out of the fourth portal she comes out seven days, so that she comes out of the fifth, and returns again in seven days into the fourth portal and completes all her light, and recedes and enters the first portal in eight days.

8. And she returns again in seven days to the fourth portal, through which the sun comes forth.

9. Thus I saw their places, the sun rising and setting according to the order of their months.

10. And in those days, if five years are taken together, the sun has thirty superabundant days; and all the days which belong to him for one of these five years, when they are full, are three hundred and sixty-four days.

11. And the superabundance of the sun and of the stars is six days; of five years, each at six, are thirty days, and the moon recedes from the sun and the stars thirty days.

12. And the moon brings in all the years exact so that their place neither precedes nor recedes ONE day, but she changes the years with exact justice in three hundred and sixty-four days.

13. Three years have one thousand and ninety-two days; and five years, eighteen hundred and twenty days; so that there will be in eight years two thousand nine hundred and twelve days.

14. To the moon alone belongs for three years one thousand and sixty-two days, and for five years she recedes fifty days, viz. to the sum of these are added sixty-two days.

15. And thus in five years, there will be seventeen hundred and seventy days, so that the days of the moon for eight years will be two thousand eight hundred and thirty-two days.

16. For her receding in eight years is eighty days, and all the days she remains behind in eight years are eighty days.

17. And the year is justly finished, in accordance with their stations and the stations of the sun, rising through their portals, through which they rise and set thirty days.

CHAPTER 75

1. And the leaders of the heads of the thousands, who are over all creation and over all the stars, are also with the four intercalary days, which cannot be separated from their places, according to the whole reckoning of the years, and these serve the four days which are not counted in the reckoning of the years.

2. And on their account men make a mistake in them, for these luminaries serve in reality on the stations of the world, one in the first portal and one in the third portal and one in the fourth portal and one in the sixth portal; and the harmony of the course of the world is brought about by its separate three hundred and sixty-four stations.

3. For the signs and the times and the years and the days, these the angel Uriel showed to me, he whom the eternal Lord of glory had placed over all the luminaries of heaven in the heavens and in the world, that they should rule on the surface of the heavens, and be seen on the earth, and be leaders for the day and for the night, viz. the sun and the moon and the stars and all the serving creatures who keep their course in all the chariots of heaven.

4. The angel Uriel showed me also twelve openings in the circuit of the chariot of the sun from which the feet [i.e. the rays] of the sun come forth; and from them comes the warmth over the earth, when they are opened at times destined for them.

5. There are also some for the winds and for the spirit of the dew, when they are opened at times, standing open in the heavens at the ends.

6. Twelve doors I saw in the heavens, in the ends of the earth, out of which come forth the sun and the moon and the stars and all the deeds of heaven, from the east and from the west.

7. And many window-openings are to the left and to the right thereof, and ONE window in its time produces warmth, like those portals from which the stars come forth as he has commanded them, and in which they set according to their number.

8. And I saw chariots in heaven, running in the world, above and below these portals, in which the stars that never set turn.

9. And one is greater than all, and this one moves through the whole world.

CHAPTER 76

1. And on the ends of the earth I saw for all the winds twelve portals opened, from which the winds come and blow over the earth.

2. Three of them are open on the face [i.e. the east] of the heavens, and three in the west, and three on the right [i.e. south] of heaven, and three on the left [i.e. north].

3. And the first three are those towards the east, and three towards the north, and three behind those which are on the left, towards the south, and three in the west.

4. Through four of these come winds of blessing and of

peace, and through those eight come winds of injury: when they are sent they bring destruction to all the earth and to the water on it and to all those who dwell on it and to everything that is in the water and on the land.

5. And the first wind from these portals, which is called the eastern, comes forth from the first portal which is towards the east, inclining towards the south; out of it comes destruction, dryness and heat and death.

6. And through the second middle portal comes forth the right mixture; there come forth rain and fruitfulness and peace and dew. And through the third portal, which is towards the north, come forth coldness and dryness.

7. And after these the winds towards the south come forth through three portals; firstly through the first portal of them, which inclines towards the east, there comes forth the wind of heat.

8. And from the middle portal, which is beside that one, there come forth a sweet incense and dew and rain and peace and life.

9. And through the third portal, which is towards the west, there come forth dew and rain and grasshoppers and destruction.

10. And after these northerly winds from the seventh portal, which is towards the east, inclining to the south, there come forth dew and rain, grasshoppers and destruction.

11. And out of the middle portal direct there come forth rain and dew and life and peace, and through the third portal, which is towards the west, which inclines towards the north, there come forth fog and hoar-frost and snow and rain and dew and grasshoppers.

12. And after these, the winds which are towards the west: through the first portal, which inclines towards the north, there come forth dew and rain and grasshoppers and coldness and snow and frost.

13. And from the middle portal there come forth dew and rain, peace and blessing, and through the last portal, which is towards the south, there come forth dryness and destruction, burning and death.

14. Thereby the twelve portals of the four portals [directions] of heaven are completed, and all their laws and all their

destructions and their virtues I showed to you, my son Methuselah.

CHAPTER 77
1. They call the first wind the eastern, because it is the first, and they call the second the southern because the Most High descends there, and especially does the Blessed One in eternity descend there.
2. And the name of the west wind is the diminishing because there the luminaries of the heavens diminish and go down.
3. And the fourth wind, called the north, is divided into three parts, one of them is for the dwelling of men, the second for the seas of water and for the valleys and for the woods and for the streams and for the darkness and for the fog; and the third part with the garden of justice.
4. I saw seven high mountains, which were higher than all the mountains which are on the earth, and from them there comes hoar-frost; and days and times and years cease and depart.
5. I saw seven rivers on the earth, larger than all the rivers; one of them coming from the west empties its water into the great sea.
6. And two of them come from the north to the sea, and empty their water into the Erythræan sea in the east.
7. But the other four come from the side of then north over to the sea, two of them to the Erythræan sea, and two empty in the great sea; according to others, in the desert.
8. I saw seven great islands in the sea and on the land: two on the land and five in the great sea.

CHAPTER 78
1. The names of the sun are these: the first Orjârês, the second Tômâs.
2. And the moon has four names: first Asônjâ, the second Eblâ, the third Benâsê, the fourth Êrâe.
3. These are the two large luminaries; their circuit is like the circuit of heaven, and in size both are equal.
4. And in the circuit of the sun there is a seventh portion of light from which some is given to the moon, and according to a measure it is added till the seventh portion of the sun is ended.

5. And they set and enter the portals of the west, and go around by the north, and come out of the portals of the east on to the surface of the heavens.

6. And when the moon is raised she is seen in the heavens, having in herself the half of the seventh part of the light, and in fourteen days her light is completed.

7. Also, three times five portions of light are put into her, so that on the fifteenth day her light is completed, according to the sign of the year, and it becomes three times five portions, and the moon becomes so by the half of the seventh part.

8. And in her decrease on the first day she decreases to fourteen parts of her light, and on the second she decreases to thirteen parts, and on the third she decreases to twelve parts, and on the fourth she decreases to eleven parts, and on the fifth she decreases to ten parts, and on the sixth she decreases to nine parts, and on the seventh she decreases to eight parts, and on the eighth she decreases to seven parts, and on the ninth she decreases to six parts, and on the tenth she decreases to five parts, and on the eleventh she decreases to four parts, and on the twelfth she decreases to three parts, and on the thirteenth she decreases to two parts, and on the fourteenth she decreases to the half of the seventh part, and her light which was left on the whole disappears altogether on the fifteenth day.

9. And in certain months the moon has each time twenty-nine days, and once twenty-eight.

10. And Uriel showed me another law, when the light is added to the moon, and from which side of the sun it is added.

11. All the time in which the moon continues in her light she increases opposite the sun, till on the fourteenth day her light is completed in heaven; and when she shines in full her light is completed in the heavens.

12. And on the first day she is called the new moon, for on that day the light is raised upon her.

13. And she is completed exactly on the day the sun descends in the west and when at night she ascends from the east and shines all night till the

sun rises opposite her and the moon is seen opposite the sun. 14. Where the light of the moon comes, there again she decreases till all her light disappears, and the days of the moon cease, and her circuit remains empty without light. 15. And three months she makes thirty days in her time and three months she makes each time twenty-nine days, in which she makes her decrease, in the first time and in the first portal for one hundred and seventy-seven days. 16. And in the time of her departure she is seen each time thirty days during three months, and each time twenty-nine days during three months. 17. At night she appears each time as a man twenty times, and during the day like the heavens, for there is nothing in her except her light.

CHAPTER 79

1. And now, my son Methuselah, I showed you all things, and the whole law of the stars is completed. 2. And he showed me all their laws for every day and for every time and for every government and for every year, and her departure,

according to her order in each month and in every week; 3. and the decrease of the moon, which takes place in the sixth portal, for in that sixth portal her light is completed, and from then there is the beginning of the month; 4. also the decrease which takes place in the first portal, in its time, till one hundred and seventy-seven days are completed; in the law of weeks, twenty-five weeks and two days; 5. and how she tarries behind the sun and according to the law of the stars five days in one time exactly; and when this place which you do see is completed. 6. This is the picture and the portrait of each luminary which the great angel Uriel, who is their leader, showed to me.

CHAPTER 80

1. And in those days Uriel answered and said to me: "Behold, I have showed you all things, O Enoch, and have revealed to you that you should see this sun and this moon, and those who lead the stars of heaven and all those that revolve, their deeds and

their times and their departures.

2. And in the days of the sinners the years will be shortened, and their seed will be tardy on their lands and on their meadows, and everything on the earth will change and will not appear in its time; the rain will be prevented, and the heavens will retain it.

3. And in those times the fruit of the earth will be tardy and will not grow in its time, and the fruit of the trees will be prevented in its time.

4. And the moon will change her order and will not appear in her time.

5. And in those days it will be seen on the heavens that a great unfruitfulness will come on the outermost chariot in the west, and she will shine more brightly that according to the order of light.

6. And many of the leaders of the stars of command will err, and they will change their paths and deeds, and those subject to them will not appear in their time.

7. And the whole order of the stars will be kept from the sinners, and the thoughts of those who dwell on the earth will err concerning them, and they will be turned from all their ways and will err and consider them gods.

8. And evil will increase over them, and punishment will come upon them to destroy them all."

CHAPTER 81

1. And he said to me: "O Enoch, contemplate the writing of the tablets of heaven, and read what is written thereon, and learn each one."

2. And I contemplated everything on these tablets of heaven, and read everything that was written, and learned everything and read the book and everything that was written in it, all the deeds of men and all the children of the flesh who will be on the earth to the generation of eternity.

3. And then I immediately blessed the Lord and the everlasting King of glory, that he had made all the things of the earth, and I blessed the Lord on account of his patience, and blessed him on account of the children of the world.

4. And at that time I said: "Happy the man who dies as a just and good one, concerning whom there is no book of

iniquity written, and against whom no blame is found."

5. And those three holy ones brought me and placed me on the earth before the door of my house and said to me: "Announce everything to your son Methulselah, and show to all your children that no flesh is just before the Lord, for he has created them.

6. One year we will leave you with your children, till you art again strengthened, that you may teach your children and write for them, and may testify before them all, your children; and in the second year they will lift you up out of their midst.

7. Let your heart be strong, for the good will announce justice to the good, the just will rejoice with the just and will congratulate themselves among themselves.

8. But the sinner will die with the sinner, and the renegade sink down with the renegade.

9. And those who do justice will die on account of the deeds of men, and will be gathered in on account of the deeds of the impious."

10. And in those days they completed conversing with me, and I went to my people blessing the Lord of the worlds.

CHAPTER 82

1. And now my son, Methuselah, all these things I relate to you and write for you, and I have revealed to you everything, and have given you books concerning them all: preserve, my son, Methuselah, the books from the hand of your father, and give them to the generations of the world.

2. Wisdom I have given you and your children and those who will be your children, that they give it to their children, the generations to eternity, namely this wisdom above their thoughts.

3. And those who understand it will not sleep, but will hear with their ears, that they may learn this wisdom, and it will please those who eat of it more than good food.

4. Happy are all the just, happy all those who walk in the paths of justice and have no sin like the sinners, in the counting of all their days, in which the sun goes through the heavens, entering and departing from the gates, each time thirty times, together with the heads of the thousands of this order of the stars, together with the

four that are added and separate between the four portions of the year, which they lead and enter with them four days.

5. And on their account, men will be at fault, and will not count them in the reckoning of the whole world; but men will be mistaken and will not know them exactly.

6. For they belong to the reckoning of the year and are exactly marked forever, one in the first portal and one in the third and one in the fourth and one in the sixth, and the year is completed in three hundred and sixty-four days.

7. And the account of it is true, and the marked reckoning exact; for the luminaries and the months and the festivals and the years have been shown and given to me by Uriel, to whom the Lord of all creation had given a command, in reference to me, of the host of the heavens.

8. And he has power over night and day in the heavens, that he may show light over men; the sun and the moon and the stars and all the powers of heaven which turn in their circuit.

9. And this is the order of the stars that set in their places and in their times and in their festivals and in their months.

10. And these are the names of those who lead them, who watch that they enter in their times and in their order and in their occasions and in their months and in their powers and in their positions.

11. Their four leaders who divide the four portions of the year enter first; after them the twelve leaders of the orders, who separate the months and the year into three hundred and sixty-four days, together with the heads of the thousands who divide the days; for the four intercalary days these are the leaders who separate the four parts of the years.

12. And of those heads of the thousands, one is placed between the leader and the led, back of the position, but their leader divides.

13. And these are the names of the leaders who separate the four parts of the year which are ordained: Melkeêl and Helemmêlêch, and Mêlêjal and Nârêl.

14. And the names of those they lead: Adnârêl and Ijasusâêl and Ijelumîêl, these three follow after the leaders of the orders, and one follows

after the three leaders of the orders, who follow after those leaders of positions who separate the four portions of the year.

15. In the commencement of the year Melkejâl rises first and rules, he who is called Tamaânî and sun, and all the days of his government that he rules are ninety-one days.

16. And these are the signs of the days which are seen on the earth in the days of his government: sweat and heat and anxiety, and all the trees producing fruit, and the leaves appearing on all the trees, and the harvest of wheat, and the blooming of roses, and all the flowers blooming in the fields, but the trees of winter become withered.

17. And these are the names of the leaders who are under them: Berkeêl, Zalbesâêl, and one other who is added, a head of a thousand, called Hêlojâsêph; and ended are the days of the power of this one.

18. The other leader, who is after them, is Helemmêlêk, whom they call the shining sun, and all the days of his light are ninety-one days.

19. And these are the signs of the days of the earth: burning heat, dryness, and the trees bringing their fruit to ripeness and completion, and the sheep mate and become pregnant; and all the fruit of the earth is gathered in, and everything that is in the fields; and the making of wine; this takes place in the days of his power.

20. These are the names and the orders and the subordinate leaders of those heads of the thousands: Gêdâêl and Kêêl and Hêêl, and the name of the head of a thousand, which is added to them, Asfâêl; and completed are the days of his power.

The Dreams

CHAPTER 83

1. And now, my son Methuselah, I will show you all the visions that I have seen, relating them before you.

2. Two visions I saw before I took a wife, and the one of them was not similar to the other; the first time, when I was learning to write, the second time, before I took your mother I saw an awful vision; and on their account, I petitioned to the Lord.

3. As I was reposing in the house of Malâlêl, my grandfather, I saw there in a vision that the heavens were lowered and disappeared and fell on the earth.

4. And as it fell on the earth I saw the earth that it was devoured in a great abyss, and mountains descended on mountains, and hills sank upon hills, and high trees were torn from the trunks, and fell down and sank into the abyss.

5. And on account of this a speech fell into my mouth, and I began to cry and to say: "The earth is destroyed!"

6. And Malâlêl, my grandfather, aroused me, as I was reposing near him, and said to me: "Why do you cry so, my son, and why do you lament so?"

7. And I related to him the whole vision which I had seen, and he said to me: "A terrible thing you have seen, my son, and the power of the vision of your dream is concerning the secrets of all the sins of the earth; it will be about to descend into the abyss and be destroyed terribly.

8. And now, my son, arise and petition the Lord of glory—

since you art a believer—that a remnant may remain on the earth and all the earth be not destroyed.

9. My son, from heaven all this will come on the earth, and over the earth, there will be great destruction."

10. After that, I arose and prayed and petitioned, and wrote down my prayer for the generations of the world, and I will show you everything, my son, Methuselah.

11. And as I went out below, and looked at the heavens and the sun rising in the east, and the moon descending in the west, and some few stars, and everything as he had known it from the first, I blessed the Lord of the judgment, and to him I gave greatness, because he led forth the sun from the windows of the east, and he ascends and rises on the surface of the heavens, and elevates himself, and goes the path which is shown to him.

CHAPTER 84

1. And I raised my hands in justice, and blessed the Holy and the Great One, and I spoke with the breath of my mouth and with the tongue of flesh, which God has made for the children of men, that they should speak with it, and gave them breath and the tongue and the mouth, that they might speak therewith:

2. "Blessed art you, O Lord, King both great and powerful in your greatness, the Lord of all the creation of heaven, King of kings, and God of all the world, your Godship and your kingdom and your greatness will remain in eternity, and to all eternity, and to all the generations your power and all the heavens are your throne in eternity, and all the earth your footstool in eternity and to all eternity.

3. For you have made and do govern all things, and nothing is too difficult for you, and no wisdom escapes you; she does not turn away from her throne, your throne, and not from your face, and you do know and see and hear all things, and there is nothing that is hidden before you, for you do see all things.

4. And now the angels of your heavens do sin, and your wrath is over the flesh of men to the day of the great judgment.

5. And now, God and Lord and great King, I petition and ask that you would establish my prayer for me, that there

remain to me a posterity on earth, and that you would not annihilate all the flesh of men, and not make empty the whole earth, and there be everlasting destruction.

6. And now, my Lord, annihilate from the earth the flesh which has angered you, but the flesh of justice and of rectitude establish as a plant of the seed to eternity, and do not hide your face from the prayer of your servant, O Lord!"

CHAPTER 85

1. And after this, I saw another dream, and I will show you all, my son.

2. And Enoch began and said to his son Methuselah: "To you, my son, I will speak; hear my words, and lend your ear to the vision of the dream of your father.

3. Before I took your mother Ednâ, I saw in a vision on my couch, and behold, a bullock came out of the earth, and this bullock was white; and after him there came a female of the same species, and together with this one came other cattle, one of them was black and one red.

4. And that black one-horned the red one, and followed it

over the earth, and then I could no longer see that red one.

5. And that black one grew, and a cow came with it, and I saw that many cattle, like it and following it, came from it.

6. And that cow, the first one, came from the presence of that first bullock, seeking that red one, and did not find it, and then raised a great cry, and hunted it.

7. And I looked until that first bullock came to her and quieted her, and from that time she did not cry aloud.

8. And after that, she brought forth another white bullock, and after that she brought forth many bullocks and black cows.

9. And I saw in my sleep that white bullock grew and become a large white bullock, and from him came many white bullocks, and they were similar to him.

10. And they commenced to beget many white bullocks, and these were similar to them, and one followed the other.

CHAPTER 86

1. And again I saw with my eyes, while I was sleeping, and I saw the heavens above, and

behold one star fell from heaven, and arose and ate and pastured among those bullocks.

2. And after that, I saw the large and the black bullocks, and behold all changed their stalls and their pastures and their cattle, and began to lament one with the other.

3. And again I saw in the vision, and looked at the heavens, and behold I saw many stars; and they fell from heaven, and were thrown from heaven near that first star, and among those cattle and bullocks; there they were with them, pasturing among them.

4. And I looked at them, and behold they all let out their sexual members, like horses, and began to mount the cows of the bullocks; and these all became pregnant, and brought forth elephants and camels and asses.

5. And all the bullocks feared them, and were affrighted at them, and they commenced to bite with their teeth, and to devour, and to push with their horns.

6. And they then began to devour those bullocks, and behold all the children of the earth began to tremble, and to shake before them, and fled.

CHAPTER 87

1. And again I saw them as they began to horn each other, and to devour each other, and the earth began to cry aloud.

2. And I again raised my eyes to heaven, and saw in the vision, and behold there came from heaven those who were like white men: one came out from that place, and three with him.

3. And those three who came out last took me by the hand, and bore me away from the generations of the earth, and elevated me to a large place, and showed me a tower higher than the earth, and all the hills were lower.

4. And they said to me: "Remain here until you see everything that comes over those elephants and camels and asses, and over the stars, and over all the bullocks."

CHAPTER 88

1. And I saw one of those four who had come out before, and he took that star which had first fallen from heaven, and bound it hand and foot, and put it in an abyss; and this abyss was narrow and deep and terrible and dark.

2. And one of them drew his sword, and gave it to those elephants and camels and asses; and they began to beat one another, and the whole earth shook on their account. 3. And as I saw in the vision, behold then one of those four who had descended threw from heaven, and gathered and took all the great stars, whose sexual members were like the sexual members of horses, and bound them all hand and foot, and put them in an abyss of the earth.

CHAPTER 89

1. And one of those four went to that white bullock, and taught him a mystery while he was trembling; he was born a bullock and became a man, and he made for himself a large vessel and lived in it; and three bullocks lived with him in that vessel, and it was covered over above them. 2. And I again raised my eyes towards heaven, and saw a high roof and seven sluices to it, and those sluices emptied much water into a yard. 3. And I saw again, and behold fountains were opened on the earth, in that great yard; and that water began to swell, and to be lifted above the land, and caused that yard to disappear, until all the land was covered with water. 4. And the water and the darkness and the fog increased over it; and as I looked at the height of this water, this water was elevated over that yard, and emptied over the yard, and stood on the earth. 5. And all the bullocks which were in the yard were collected, so that I immediately saw how they sank down and came to naught, and were destroyed in that water. 6. But that vessel swam on the water, and all the bullocks and elephants and camels and asses on the earth sank down, and all the animals; and I was not able to see them, and they were unable to come out, but were destroyed, and sank down into the abyss. 7. And again I saw in the vision till those sluices were put away from that high roof, and the fountains of the earth dried up, and other abysses were opened. 8. Then the water began to run into these till the earth became uncovered; but that vessel reached the earth, and the darkness retreated, and it became light.

9. But that white bullock, which had become a man, came out of that vessel, and the three bullocks with him; and one of the three bullocks was white, similar to that [first] bullock, and one of them was red like blood, and one black; and that one, the white bullock, went away from them.

10. And they began to bring forth animals of the desert and birds, so that there arose out of them a varied diversity of kinds: lions and panthers and dogs and wolves and hyenas and wild boars and foxes and squirrels and hogs and falcons and vultures and buzzards and eagles and crows; and among them was born a white bullock.

11. And they began to bite one another, but that white bullock which was born among them begat a wild ass and a white bullock with it, and the wild ass increased.

12. But that bull which was born from him begat a black wild boar and a white sheep, and this wild boar begat many boars, but that sheep produced twelve sheep.

13. And when these twelve sheep had grown, they gave one of them to the asses, and these asses then gave that sheep to the wolves, and that sheep grew up among the wolves.

14. And the Lord brought the eleven sheep to live with it, and to pasture with it among the wolves, and they increased, and became many herds of sheep.

15. And the wolves began to fear, and oppressed them till they [the wolves] finally destroyed their [i.e. the sheep's] young, and threw their young into a stream of much water; but these sheep began to cry aloud, on account of their young, before the Lord.

16. And a sheep which had been saved from the wolves fled, and escaped to the wild asses; and I saw the sheep as they lamented and cried and asked their Lord with all their power, till that Lord of the sheep descended at the voice of the sheep from his high abode, and came and looked after them.

17. And he called to that sheep which had escaped from the wolves, and spoke with it concerning the wolves, that it should counsel them not to touch the sheep.

18. And that sheep went to the wolves by the voice of the

Lord; and another sheep met that sheep, and went with it, and these two came together to the abode of those wolves, and spoke with them, and admonished them that from this moment they should not touch the sheep.

19. And then I saw the wolves, and how they exceedingly oppressed the sheep with all their power; and the sheep cried aloud.

20. And their Lord came to the sheep, and began to beat those wolves, and the wolves began to lament; but the sheep became quiet, and from then on did not cry.

21. And I saw the sheep till they had gone away from the wolves, and the wolves were blinded as to their eyes, and those wolves went out that they might follow the sheep with all their power.

22. And the Lord of the sheep went with them, leading them, and all the sheep followed him; and his face was shining, and this appearance terrible and sublime.

23. But the wolves commenced to follow those sheep till they reached them in a sea of water.

24. And this sea of water was divided, and the water stood from this side and from that before their faces; and their Lord leading them stood also between them and the wolves.

25. And as those wolves did not yet see the sheep, they went into the middle of the sea of water; and the wolves followed the sheep, and ran after them into the sea of water.

26. And when they saw the Lord of the sheep they turned that they might flee from before his face; but this sea of water gathered itself together, suddenly took again its own character, and the water swelled and rose till it covered those wolves.

27. And I saw till all the wolves which had followed those sheep were destroyed, and sank down.

28. But the sheep escaped from that water, and went into the desert, where there was no water and no grass; and they began to open their eyes and to see; and I saw the Lord of the sheep pasturing them and giving them water and grass, and that [former] sheep going and leading them.

29. And this sheep ascended to the height of a high rock, and the Lord of the sheep sent it to them.

30. And after that I saw the Lord of the sheep as he stood before them; and his appearance was terrible and powerful, and all those sheep saw him, and were afraid before his face.

31. And they were all afraid, and trembled before him, and cried after that sheep which was with him to the other sheep which was among them: "We are not able to exist before our Lord, or to look at him."

32. And that sheep which led them returned, and ascended to the height of that rock; but the sheep began to be blinded as to their eyes and erred from the path which it showed to them, but this sheep did not know it.

33. And the Lord of the sheep was enraged over them greatly, and that sheep discovered it, and descended from the height of the rock, and came to the sheep, and found the greater part of them blinded as to their eyes, and erring from his path.

34. And as they saw it they feared and trembled before its face, and desired to return to their folds.

35. And that sheep took other sheep with it, and came to those erring sheep; and then it began to kill them, and the sheep feared its countenance; and thus that sheep brought back those erring sheep, and they returned to their folds.

36. And I saw there in the vision till that sheep became a man, and built the Lord of the sheep a house, and placed all the sheep in that house.

37. And I saw till that sheep that had met the sheep which led the sheep reposed [in death], and I saw till all the large sheep were destroyed, and small ones arose in their places, and they came to a pasture and approached a stream of water.

38. And this sheep which led them, and which became a man, was separated from them, and reposed [in death]; and all the sheep sought it, and cried over it exceedingly.

39. And I saw till they became quiet from their crying over this sheep, and they crossed that stream of water, and there always arose other sheep that led them in the place of those which had departed and led them.

40. And I saw the sheep until they came into a good place, and into a pleasant and glorious land; and I saw these

sheep till they were satisfied, but the house stood among them in the beautiful land.

41. And sometimes their eyes were opened, and sometimes they were blinded, till another sheep arose, and led them, and conducted them all back, and their eyes were opened.

42. And the dogs and the foxes and the wild boars began to devour those sheep till another sheep arose, a buck, in their midst, which led them.

43. And this buck began to butt those dogs and those foxes and those wild boars from both sides, till he had destroyed them all.

44. And that sheep had its eyes opened, and saw this buck which was among the sheep departing from his honor, and beginning to butt those sheep, and to tramp on them, and to walk unseemly.

45. And the Lord of the sheep sent that sheep to another sheep and exalted it to become a buck, and to lead the sheep in the place of that sheep which had deserted his honor.

46. And it went to it, and spoke to it alone, and elevated it to become a buck, and made it the prince and leader of the sheep; but during all that time

those dogs oppressed the sheep.

47. And the first buck pursued the second buck, and the second buck rose up and fled before its face, and I saw till those dogs cast down the first buck.

48. And that second buck arose, and led the smaller sheep, and this buck begat many sheep, and reposed [in death], and a small sheep became the buck in its place and was the prince and leader of those sheep.

49. And those sheep grew and increased, and the dogs and the foxes and the wild boars were afraid and fled before it, and that buck butted and killed all the wild beasts, and those wild beasts had no more power among the sheep, and never robbed them of anything.

50. And that house became great and broad, and a large tower was built on that house of the Lord of the sheep for those sheep, and the house was low, but the tower was high and broad, and the Lord of the sheep stood on that tower, and they placed a full table before him.

51. And I again saw those sheep that they again erred,

and went many ways, and left their house, and the Lord of the sheep called some from among them, and sent them to the sheep, but the sheep began to kill them.

52. And one of them was saved, and was not killed, but escaped, and cried over the sheep, and they wanted to kill it, but the Lord of the sheep saved it out of the hands of the sheep, and brought it up to me, and caused it to dwell there.

53. And he sent many other sheep to those sheep to admonish them, and to lament over them.

54. And after that I saw, as they left the house of the Lord of the sheep and his tower, they departed entirely, and their eyes were blinded; and I saw the Lord of the sheep that he caused much death among them in each one of their herds, till these sheep even called for this death, and they betrayed his place.

55. And he left them in the hand of the lions and tigers and wolves and jackals, and in the hand of foxes and all the wild beasts, and these wild beasts began to tear those sheep to pieces.

56. And I saw that he left that house of theirs and their tower and gave them all into the hand of lions that they should tear and devour them, into the hand of all the wild beasts.

57. And I began to cry aloud with all my power, and called upon the Lord of the sheep and showed him this in reference to the sheep, that they were being devoured by all the wild beasts.

58. But he remained silent, seeing it, and rejoiced that they were devoured and swallowed and robbed, and left them in the hand of all the wild beasts as food.

59. And he called seventy shepherds and put away those sheep, in order that they should pasture them, and he spoke to the shepherds and to their companions: "Each single one of you will now pasture the sheep, and everything I command you, do!

60. And I deliver them over to you according to number, and will tell you which of them will be destroyed; those kill!"

61. And he gave those sheep over to them. And to another, he called and said to him: "Watch and see everything that the shepherds do

concerning these sheep; for they will destroy more of them than I have commanded.

62. And each superabundance and the destruction which the shepherds do to these write down, how many they destroy by my command, and how many they destroy by their own will, and write down separately each destruction by each shepherd.

63. And according to the number recite before me how many they have destroyed of their own account and how many were given them for destruction, that this may be a testimony for me against them, that I may know every deed of the shepherds to give them over, and may see what they do, whether they do my commands which I have commanded them or not.

64. And they will not know, and you shalt not let them know nor admonish them, but write down all the destruction of the shepherds, each one in its time, and lay everything before me."

65. And I saw till those shepherds pastured in their times and began to kill and to destroy more than was commanded them, and left those sheep in the hands of the lions.

66. And the lions and the tigers devoured and swallowed the greater part of those sheep, and the wild boars devoured with them, and they burned that tower and demolished that house.

67. And I mourned a great deal over that tower because that house of the sheep was demolished; and after that I could no longer see those sheep whether they entered that house.

68. And the shepherds and their companions delivered over those sheep to all the wild beasts to devour them, and each one of them received in his time a certain number, and of each one the other wrote down in a book how many he destroyed.

69. And each one killed and destroyed more than was ordered him, and I began to cry and to lament exceedingly concerning those sheep.

70. And in the vision I saw that scribe as he wrote each one that was destroyed by those shepherds on each day and brought up and opened and showed this whole book to the Lord of the sheep, everything that they had done

and every one that each single one had removed and every one that they had handed over for destruction,

71. And the book was read before the Lord of the sheep, and he took the book in his hand, and read it and sealed it and laid it down.

72. And after that I saw that shepherds pastured twelve hours, and behold, three of those sheep turned around and came and entered and began to build everything that was demolished of the house, but the wild boars attempted to hinder them, and they could not.

73. And they again began to build, as before, and put up that tower, and it was called "the high tower"; and they again began to place a table before that tower, and all the bread on it was unclean and not pure.

74. And concerning all this the sheep were blinded as to their eyes, and did not see, and their shepherds likewise; and a great many were delivered to their shepherds for destruction, and they trod on the sheep with their feet and devoured them.

75. And the Lord of the sheep remained quiet till all the sheep were scattered in the field and mixed themselves with them and did not save them from the hands of the wild beasts.

76. And he who wrote the book brought it to the houses of the Lord of the sheep, and showed it and read it and petitioned him on their account and asked him, while showing him all the deeds of their shepherds and testifying before him against all the shepherds.

77. And he took the book and laid it beside him, and departed.

CHAPTER 90

1. And I saw to the time when thirty-six shepherds thus pastured, and each one completed his time like the first; and others received them in their hands to pasture them in their time, each shepherd in his own time.

2. And after that I saw in the vision all the birds of heaven coming: the eagles and the vultures and the buzzards and the crows; but the eagles led all the birds; and they began to devour those sheep and to pick out their eyes and to devour their flesh.

3. And the sheep cried out because their flesh was being

devoured by the birds. And I cried and lamented in my sleep over that shepherd who was pasturing the sheep.

4. And I saw until those sheep were devoured by the dogs and the eagles and the buzzards, and they did not leave on them meat or skin or muscles till the skeletons stood there alone, and the skeletons fell to the ground also, and the sheep became less.

5. And I saw to the time when twenty-three shepherds pastured, and they completed, each in his time, fifty-eight times.

6. But small lambs were born from those white sheep, and they began to open their eyes and to see and to cry to the sheep.

7. But the sheep did not cry to them and did not hear what they said to them, but were exceedingly deaf, and their eyes exceedingly and powerfully blinded.

8. And I saw in the vision that the crows flew on to those lambs and took one of those lambs, but broke the sheep and devoured them.

9. And I saw till horns came to those lambs and the crows threw down those horns; and I saw till ONE great horn came

forth, ONE of those sheep, and their eyes were opened.

10. And it looked at them, and their eyes were opened, and it cried to the sheep, and the bucks saw it, and all ran to it.

11. And with all that those eagles and vultures and crows and buzzards to that time were tearing those sheep to pieces, and flew down on them and devoured them; but the sheep remained quiet, and the bucks lamented and cried out.

12. And those crows fought and battled with it and sought to remove that horn, but had no power over it.

13. And I saw them till the shepherds and the eagles and those vultures and buzzards came, and they cried to those crows that they should break that horn of the buck; and they fought and battled with it, and it fought with them and cried that its help might come to it.

14. And I saw till that man who had written down the names of the shepherds and brought them up to the Lord of the sheep came, and he helped that buck and showed it everything, that its help had come down.

15. And I saw till that Lord of the sheep came to them in

anger, and all who saw him fled, and all fell into his shadow before his face.

16. All the eagles and vultures and crows and buzzards assembled and brought with them all the sheep of the desert, and they all came together and assisted one another in order to break that horn of the buck.

17. And I saw that man who had written the book by the voice of God till he opened that book of destruction which those last twelve shepherds had practiced, and showed that they had destroyed more that those before them, before the Lord of the sheep.

18. And I saw till the Lord of the sheep came to them and took the rod of anger in his hand, and struck the earth so that the earth was rent apart, and all the beasts and the birds of heaven fell away from those sheep, and sank down into the earth, and it was covered over them.

19. And I saw till a great sword was given to the sheep, and the sheep came to those wild beasts to kill them, and all the beasts and the birds of heaven fled from their face.

20. And I saw till a throne was built on the earth in the pleasant land, and the Lord of the sheep sat upon it, and he took all the sealed books and opened those books before the Lord of the sheep.

21. And the Lord called to those first six white ones, and commanded that they should bring to him, from the first star on, which had come forth, all the stars whose sexual members had been similar to the sexual members of horses, and also the first star that had first fallen; and they brought all before him.

22. And he said to that man who wrote before him, who was one of the six white ones, and said to him: "Take those seventy shepherds to whom I have delivered the sheep, and taking them, they of their own account killed more than I had commanded them."

23. And behold I saw them all bound, and all stood before him.

24. And the judgment was first over the stars, and they were judged and were found to be sinners, and went to the place of judgment and were thrown into an abyss filled with fire and burning and filled with pillars of fire.

25. And those seventy shepherds were judged and were found to be sinners, and THEY were thrown into this abyss of fire.

26. And I saw at that time that an abyss like it was opened in the middle of the earth, which was full of fire, and they brought those blinded sheep, and they all were judged and were found to be sinners, and were thrown into the abyss of fire and burned; and this abyss was to the right of that house.

27. And I saw those sheep burning, and their bones burned.

28. And I stood looking till he enveloped that old house, and they took out all the pillars, and all the planks and the ornaments of that house were wrapped in with it, and they brought it out and put it in one place, on the right [i.e. south] of the earth.

29. And I saw the Lord of the sheep till he produced a new house, larger and higher than that first, and put it in the place of the first, which had been enveloped, and all its pillars were new, and the ornaments new and larger than of the first old one, which he had removed, and all the sheep were in its middle.

30. And I saw all the sheep that had been left and all the animals on the earth and all the birds of the heavens, falling down and worshiping those sheep and petitioning and obeying them in every word.

31. And after that those three who were dressed in white, who had led me up before, took me by the hand, and the hand of that buck taking hold of me, they raised me, and put me down in the midst of those sheep before the judgment took place.

32. But those sheep were all white, and their wool large and clean.

33. And all that were destroyed and scattered, and all the wild beasts and all the birds of heaven were collected in that house, and the Lord of the sheep rejoiced greatly, for they were all good and had returned to his house.

34. And I saw till they laid down that sword which had been given to the sheep, and returned it to his house; and it was sealed before the face of the Lord, and all the sheep were closed up in that house, but it could not contain them.

35. And the eyes of all of them were opened, and they saw the

good, and there was not ONE among them that did not see.
36. And I saw that that house was large and broad and exceedingly full.
37. And I saw that a white bullock was born, and his horns were large, and all the wild beasts and all the birds of heaven feared him and petitioned him at all times.
38. And I saw till all their generations were changed, and they all became white bullocks, and the first one of them [was the word, and that word] was a great animal, and had on its head large and black horns; and the Lord of the sheep rejoiced over them and over all the bullocks.
39. And I reposed in their midst, and I awoke and saw everything.
40. And this is the vision that I saw as I was asleep; and I awoke and blessed the Lord of justice and gave him glory.
41. And then I cried greatly, and my tears did not stand still till I was not able to endure it; when I looked they flowed on account of that which I saw, because everything will come and be fulfilled, and all the deeds of men in their order appeared to me.
42. And in that night I remembered my first dream, and on its account, I cried and trembled, because I had seen that vision.

The Epistle of Enoch

CHAPTER 91

1. And now, my son Methuselah, call to me all your brothers, and assemble to me all the children of your mother, for the word calls me, and the spirit is poured out over me, that I show you all that will happen to you to eternity.

2. And then Methuselah went and called all his brothers to him and assembled his relatives.

3. And he conversed with all his children concerning justice, and said: "Hear, my children, all the words of your father, and listen properly to the voice of my mouth, for I admonish you and tell you, my beloved, love rectitude and walk in it.

4. And do not approach rectitude with a double heart, and do not associate with those of a double heart, but walk in justice, my children, and she will lead you in the good path, and justice will be your companion.

5. For I know that a condition of oppression will grow strong on the earth, and great punishment will be completed over the earth, and all injustice will be completed and be cut off by the roots, and its whole habitation destroyed.

6. And again injustice will be repeated, and all the deeds of injustice and the deeds of oppression and of sin will be renewed on the earth.

7. And when injustice and sin and reviling and oppression and all the deeds will increase, and falling-off and reviling and uncleanness will increase; there will be a great

punishment from heaven upon them all, and the holy Lord will come forth in anger, and with punishment, that he may pass judgment on the earth.

8. And in those days oppression will be cut off from its roots, and the roots of injustice together with deception, and they will be destroyed from under heaven.

9. And all the pictures of the heathens will be given away; the towers will be burned by fire, and they will be removed from the whole earth, and will be thrown into a condemnation of fire, and will be destroyed in anger, and in a strong judgment which will be to eternity.

10. And the just one will arise from sleep, and wisdom will arise and will be given to them.

11. And then the roots of injustice will be cut off, and the sinners will be destroyed with the sword, and the roots of the revilers will be cut off in every place, and those who contemplate oppression and revile will be destroyed by the edge of the sword.

12. And after that there will be another week, the eighth, that of justice, and the sword will be given to it, that it may pass judgment and justice on those who practice injustice, and the sinners will be delivered into the hands of the just.

13. And in the end of it they will acquire houses through their justice, and they will build a house to the Great King as an honor to eternity.

14. And after that, in the ninth week, the judgment of justice will be revealed to all the world, and all the doings of the impious will depart from the world, and the world will be written out for destruction, and all men will look for the path of rectitude.

15. And after this, in the tenth week, in the seventh part, there will be the judgment to eternity, which is held over the watchers and the great heavens of eternity which will spring forth from the midst of the angels.

16. And the first heaven will pass away and cease, and a new heaven will appear, and all the powers of heaven will shine to eternity sevenfold.

17. And after that, there will be many weeks, without number, to eternity, in goodness and in justice, and sin will not be mentioned

from that time on to eternity.—

18. And now I tell you, my children, and show you the paths of justice and the paths of oppression, and I will show them to you again that ye may know what will come.

19. And now hear, my children, and walk in the paths of justice, and do not walk in the paths of oppression, for they will be destroyed in eternity who walk in the paths of injustice.

CHAPTER 92

1. Written by Enoch, the scribe, all this doctrine of wisdom, praiseworthy to all men, and a judge of all the earth, to all my children who will dwell on the earth, and to the future generations who will practice rectitude and peace.

2. Let not your spirits be sorrowful on account of the times, for the Great Holy One has given days for everything.

3. And the just one will arise from sleep, will arise and walk in the paths of justice, and all his ways will be in everlasting goodness and grace.

4. He will be gracious to the just one, and will give him everlasting rectitude and will give power, and will be in goodness and justice, and he will walk in the everlasting light.

5. But sin will be destroyed in darkness to eternity, and will not be seen from that day on to eternity.

CHAPTER 93

1. And after that Enoch commenced to relate out of the books.

2. And Enoch said: "Concerning the children of justice and concerning the chosen of the world and concerning the plant of justice and of rectitude, of these I will speak to you and announce to you, my children, I, Enoch, as it has appeared to me in a vision from heaven, and what I learned through the voice of the holy angels and understood from the tablets of heaven."

3. And Enoch commenced to relate from the books and said: "I was born the seventh in the first week, while judgment and justice were yet retarded.

4. And there will arise after me in the second week great evil, and destruction will spring up, and in it there will be the first end, and in it a man will be saved; and after it is finished

injustice will grow, and he will make a law for the sinners.

5. And after that, in the third week, in the end thereof, a man will be chosen as a plant of the judgment of justice, and after him, the plant of justice will come forever.

6. And after that, in the fourth week, in the end thereof, visions of the holy and the just will be seen, and a law for all generations and a court will be made for them.

7. And after that, in the fifth week, in the end thereof, a house of glory and of supremacy will be built to eternity.

8. And after that, in the sixth week, those who will exist in it will all be blinded, and their hearts will all forget wisdom, and in it a man will ascend; and in the end thereof the house of supremacy will burn with fire, and the whole race of the chosen root will be cut off.

9. And after that, in the seventh week, a rebellious generation will arise, and many will be their deeds, and all their deeds will be rebellious.

10. And in the end thereof the chosen just of the everlasting plant of justice will be rewarded; seven portions of learning are given to them concerning all his creatures.

11. And who is there of all the children of men that is able to hear the voice of the Holy One, and does not tremble, and who is able to think his thoughts, and who that is able to see all the works of heaven?

12. And how could one know the deeds of heaven and be able to see his breath and his spirit, and be able to relate it, or ascend and see all their ends, and think them or act like them?

13. And who is the man that is able to know what the breadth and the length of the earth is, and to whom has the measure of them all been shown?

14. Or is there any man who is able to know the length of heaven, and what is its height, and upon what it is established, and what is the measure as regards the number of the stars, and where all the luminaries rest?

CHAPTER 94

1. And now I say to you, my children, love justice and walk in it, for the paths of justice are worthy that they be accepted; and the paths of injustice are destroyed suddenly and cease.

2. And to certain men of a future generation, the paths of violence and of death will be revealed, and they will retreat from them, and will not follow them.

3. And now I say to you, the just: Do not walk in the wicked path and in violence, and not in the paths of death, and do not approach them, that ye be not destroyed.

4. But love and choose for yourselves justice and a pleasing life, and walk in the paths of peace, that you may live and have joy.

5. And hold in the thoughts of your hearts, and let not my words be eradicated from your hearts, for I know that the sinners will deceive men to make wisdom wicked, and it [i.e. wisdom] will not find a place, and all kinds of temptations will not cease.

6. Woe to those who build injustice and violence, and found deception, for they will be rooted out suddenly, and will have no peace.

7. Woe to those who build their houses in sin, for they will be rooted out from their foundation, and will fall by the sword; and they who acquire gold and silver will be destroyed by sudden judgment.

8. Woe to you rich, for you have trusted in your riches, but you will come away from your riches because you have not remembered the Most High in the days of your riches.

9. You have done reviling and injustice, and were prepared for the day of bloodshed, and for the day of darkness, and for the day of the great judgment.

10. Thus I speak to you, and announce to you that he who has created you will destroy you from the foundation, and over your fall there will be no pity, and your Creator will rejoice in your destruction.

11. And your just in those days will be a disgrace to sinners and the impious.

CHAPTER 95

1. Oh that my eyes were clouds of water, and I could weep over you, and pour out my tears like a cloud of water, and I could rest from the sorrow of my heart.

2. Who has empowered you to practice hate and wickedness? May the judgment reach you, the sinners!

3. Fear not the sinners, you just, for God will give them into your hands again, that you may pass judgment over them, as you desire.

4. Woe to you who pronounce curses that they be not loosened, and healing will be far from you on account of your sins!

5. Woe to you who repay evil to your neighbor, for you will be repaid according to your deeds!

6. Woe to you, the witnesses of untruth, and to those who weigh injustice, for you will be destroyed suddenly.

7. Woe to you sinners, for you pursue the just; for you will be given over and pursued, you men of injustice, and heavy will be their yokes upon you.

CHAPTER 96

1. Hope, you just, for the sinners will be destroyed suddenly before you, and the power over them will be to you as you desire.

2. And in the day of the trouble of the sinners your children will mount and rise like eagles, and your nest will be higher than the hawk, and you will ascend and go like the squirrels into the recesses of the earth, and into the clefts of the rock to eternity, before the unjust; but they will lament over you, and cry like satyrs.

3. But fear not, you who suffer, for a healing will be to you, and a brilliant light will shine for you, and you will hear the voice of rest from heaven.

4. Woe to you, sinners, for your riches make you appear like the just, but your hearts prove to you that you are sinners; and this word will be a testimony against you, as a remembrance of wicked deeds.

5. Woe to you who devour the marrow of the wheat, and drink the power of the root of the fountain, and trod down the lowly by your power.

6. Woe to you who drink water at all times, for you will be repaid suddenly and will dry up and wilt because you have left the fountain of life.

7. Woe to you who practice injustice and destruction and reviling; there will be a remembrance against you for evil.

8. Woe to you powerful, who throw down with power the just ones, for the day of your destruction will come. In those days many and good days will come to the just, on the day of your judgment.

CHAPTER 97

1. Believe, you just, for the sinners will come to shame, and will be destroyed on the day of injustice.

2. It will be known to you that the Most High is mindful of your destruction, and the angels rejoice over your destruction.

3. What will you do, you sinners, and where will you flee, on that day of judgment, when you will hear the voice of the prayer of the just?

4. You will not be like those, you against whom this word will be a testimony: "You have been companions of the sinners."

5. And in those days, the prayer of the just will reach the Lord, and the days of your judgment will come to you.

6. And all the words of your injustice will be recited before the Great and Holy One; and your faces will be filled with shame, and each work that is founded on injustice will be cast off.

7. Woe to you sinners, in the midst of the ocean and over the land whose remembrance of you is evil!

8. Woe to you who acquire silver and gold without justice, and say: "We have become rich, and have treasures, and possess everything we desire;

9. And now we will do what we contemplate, for we have gathered together silver, and our treasuries are filled, and as water so many are the workmen of our houses."

10. And like water your lies will float away, for wealth will not remain for you, but will ascend suddenly from you, for you have acquired it all in injustice, and you will be given over to a great condemnation.

CHAPTER 98

1. And now I swear to you, the wise and the foolish; for you will see much on this earth.

2. For men will put on more ornaments than the women, and colored garments more than the virgin; in royalty, and in greatness, and in power, and in silver, and in gold, and purple and honor, and in food, they will float away like water.

3. And therefore they will have no knowledge and no wisdom, and thereby they are destroyed together with their treasures, and with all their glory and their honor, and in shame and in murder and in great poverty

their spirits will be cast into an oven of fire.

4. I swear to you sinners: as a mountain has not and will not become a slave, nor a hill the maid of a woman, for sin was not sent to the earth, but mankind themselves have created it, and it will be for a great curse to those who do it.

5. And barrenness has not been given to a woman, but on account of the deeds of her hands she dies without children.

6. I swear to you sinners, by the Holy and the Just One, that all your wicked deeds are revealed in the heavens, and none of your deeds of violence are covered or hidden.

7. And do not think in your souls, and do not say in your hearts, that you do not know and do not see that every sin is daily being written down in heaven before the Most High.

8. And from now you know that all your violence which you commit is written down on each day to the day of your judgment.

9. Woe to you fools for you will be destroyed by your foolishness, and you do not listen to the wise, and will not attain anything good!

10. And now know that you are prepared for the day of destruction, and do not hope that you will live, you sinners, but you will depart and die, for you do not know a ransom; for you are prepared for the day of the great judgment, and for the day of trouble and of great disgrace to your souls.

11. Woe to you hardened of heart, who do evil and devour blood; from where is your good eating and drinking and satisfaction? from all the good which our Lord the Most High has spread in abundance over the earth; and you will have no peace.

12. Woe to you who love the deeds of injustice; why do you hope for goodness to yourselves? Know that you will be given into the hands of the just; they will cut off your necks and slay you, and will not pity you.

13. Woe to you who rejoice in the trouble of the just, for a grave will not be dug for you.

14. Woe to you who make the words of the just in vain, for the hope of life will not be to you.

15. Woe to you who write down words of untruth and words of the impious; for they write down their lies that they

be heard, and do not forget their foolishness, and there will be no peace to them, but they will die a sudden death!

CHAPTER 99

1. Woe to those who act impiously, and glory in the words of untruth, and honor them; you will be destroyed, and will have no good life.
2. Woe to you who change the words of rectitude, and who transgress the law of eternity, and make themselves that which they are not, namely, sinners; they will be tramped down on the earth.
3. And in those days prepare yourselves, you just, to raise your prayers of remembrance, and you will place them as a testimony before the angels, that they may lay the sins of the sinners before the Most High as a remembrance.
4. In those days the nations will be disturbed, and the generations of the nations will arise on the day of destruction.
5. And in those days the fruit of the womb will miscarry, and they will mangle their own children, and they will cast their children from them, and miscarriages will pass from them; they will cast infants from them, and will not return

to them, and will not pity their beloved.
6. Again I swear to you sinners, that sin has been prepared for a day of blood which does not end.
7. And they will worship stones; and others will make images of gold and of silver and of wood and of clay, and others will worship unclean spirits and demons and all kinds of idols, even in the idol temples; but no help will be found in them.
8. And they will become impious in the foolishness of their hearts, and their eyes will be blinded through fear in their hearts and through a vision of their dreams.
9. Through them they will be impious and will fear, because they do all their deeds in untruth, and worship stones; but they will be destroyed in an instant.
10. But in those days blessed are all they who receive the words of wisdom and know them, and do the paths of the Most High, and walk in the path of justice, and do not act impiously with those who act impiously; for they will be saved.
11. Woe to you who spread

evil among your neighbors, for you will be killed in hell.

12. Woe to you who make a foundation for sin and deception, and who cause bitterness on the earth, for thereby they will reach an end.

13. Woe to you who build your houses by the labor of another, and whose building material is nothing but the bricks and stones of sin. I tell you that you will have no peace.

14. Woe to those who cast away the measure and the inheritance of their fathers, which is forever, and cause their souls to follow after idols; no rest will be to them.

15. Woe to those who practice injustice and aid oppression, and kill their neighbors, to the day of the great judgment!

16. For he will cast down your glory, and put the wickedness to your hearts, and will raise the spirit of his anger, and will destroy you all with the sword, and all the just and holy will remember your sins.

CHAPTER 100

1. And in those days the fathers will be slain in one place with their sons, and brothers with the others will fall in death, till it flows like a stream from their blood.

2. For a man will not in mercy draw his hand from his sons, and from his sons' sons, to kill them, and the sinner will not draw his hand from his honored brother; from the dawn to the setting sun they will kill each other.

3. And a horse will walk up to his breast in the blood of the sinners, and a wagon will sink in to its height.

4. And it those days the angels will come into the secret places, and will collect in one place all those who aided sin; and the Most High will arise on that day to pass a great judgment over all the sinners.

5. But over all the just and holy he will place holy angels as watchmen to watch them like the apple of an eye, till an end has been made to evil and to all sin; and even if the holy sleep a long sleep there is nothing to fear.

6. And the wise among men will see the truth, and the children of the earth will understand all the words of this book, and know that their riches will not be able to save them in the overthrow of their sins.

7. Woe to you sinners, if you trouble the just, on the day of great pain, and burn them with fire; you will be repaid according to your work.

8. Woe to the hardened of heart, who watch to contrive wickedness: fear will be about to come over you, and there will be none to save you.

9. Woe to you sinners, for on account of the words of your mouth, and on account of the deeds of your hands, which you have done, you who act impiously will burn in a pool of flaming fire.

10. And now know that the angels will seek out your deeds in heaven from the sun and the moon and the stars in reference to your sins, because you pass judgment on the earth on the just.

11. And he will call to testify over you each cloud and fog and dew and rain, for they all will be kept back from you that they do not descend upon you; and will they not think of your sins?

12. And now give presents to the rain that it may not be kept back from descending upon you, or the dew when it has received gold or silver from you.

13. When frost and snow and their coldness descend upon you, and all the winds of the snow and all their plagues, in those days you will not be able to stand before them.

CHAPTER 101

1. Notice the heavens, all you children of heaven, and all the doings of the Most High, and have fear of him, and do no evil before him.

2. When he locks the windows of heaven, and prevents the rain and the dew from descending upon the earth on your account, what will you do then?

3. And when he sends his anger over you and over all your deeds, you cannot petition him, because you have spoken concerning his justice proudly and boldly, and you will have no peace.

4. And do you not see the kings of the ships, how their ships are chased about by waves, and tremble before the winds, and are troubled?

5. And therefore they fear, because all their good treasures go into the sea with them, and they are troubled in their hearts that the sea might swallow them and they perish in it.

6. Is not all the sea and all its waters and all its movements a work of the Most High, and has he not limited its actions, and bound it all in the sand?

7. It dries up at his threats and is afraid, and all its fish die, and all that is in it; and you sinners who are on the earth do not fear him.

8. Has he not made heaven and earth, and all that is in them? And who has given understanding and wisdom to all who move on the earth, and to those on the sea?

9. Do not the kings of the ships fear the sea? but the sinners do not fear the Most High.

CHAPTER 102

1. And in those days when he brings a painful fire upon you, were will you flee, and where will ye save yourselves? and when he brings his word upon you, will you then not be aghast and fear?

2. And all the luminaries will tremble in great fear, and all the earth will be horrified and will tremble and quake.

3. And all the angels will fulfill their commands and will desire to hide themselves from before him, great in glory, and the children of the earth will tremble and shake; and you, sinners, are cursed to eternity, and will have no peace.

4. Fear not, you souls of the just, and hope for the day of your death in justice.

5. And be not sorrowful that your souls descend into Sheol, in great trouble and lamentation and sorrow, and in grief, and that your bodies have not found it in your life as your goodness deserved, but rather on a day on which you were like the sinners, and on the day of the curse and the punishment.

6. And when you die the sinners speak over you: "As we die the just die, and what benefit have they in their deeds?

7. Behold, as we, they have died in anxiety and in darkness, and what advantage have they over us? from now on we are equal.

8. And what will they receive, and what will they see to eternity? For behold, they too have died, and from now on to eternity they do not see the light."

9. I tell you sinners: it is sufficient for you to eat and drink and to make a man naked, and to rob and to sin,

and to acquire wealth, and to see good days.

10. Have you seen the just, how their end was peace because no oppression was found in them to the day of their death?

11. "And they were destroyed and became as if they had not been, and the souls descended in Sheol in trouble."

CHAPTER 103

1. And now I swear to you the just, by his great glory and his honor, and by his glorious kingdom and by his greatness I swear to you:

2. I know this mystery, and have read it in the tablets of heaven, and have seen the book of the holy ones, and have found written in it and inscribed on their account,

3. that all goodness and joy and honor are prepared for them, and are written down for the spirits of those who have died in justice, and that much good is given to you as a reward for your labor, and that your portion is better than the portion of the living.

4. And your souls will live, you who have died in justice, and your spirits will rejoice and be glad, and their remembrance will be before the face of the Great One to all the generations of eternity. And now do not fear their shame.

5. Woe to you, sinners, if you die in your sins, and those who are like you say concerning you: "Blessed are they, the sinners, they have seen all their days;

6. and now they have died in good fortune and in wealth, and have not seen trouble or murder in their life; in glory, they have died, and judgment has not been passed over them in their life."

7. Do you know that their souls will be caused to descend into Sheol, and it will be ill with them, and their trouble great?

8. And in darkness and in toils and in a burning flame their spirits will burn at the great judgment; and a great judgment will be for all generations to eternity. Woe to you, for you will have no peace!

9. Say not to the just and good who are in life: "In the days of our need we have endured labor, and have seen all need, and have met much evil, and have been injured and diminished, and our spirit has become small.

10. We have been destroyed, and there was none to help us; with word and deed we were incapable, and attained to nothing whatever; we were tortured and destroyed, and did not hope to see life, day by day.

11. We hoped to be the head, and were the tail; we labored exceedingly, and did not gain by our labor; we became food for sinners, and the unjust laid their yoke heavily upon us.

12. Those who hated and those who beat us became our rulers, and we bent our neck to our haters, and they did not pity us.

13. And we desired to go from them in order to flee and to rest, but we did not find where to flee and to save ourselves from them.

14. We complained to the rulers in our trouble and in our pain over those who devoured us; but they did not attend to our cry, and did not wish to hear our voice.

15. And they helped those who robbed and devoured us, and those who diminished us, and they made secret their oppression, so that they did not remove their yoke from us, but devoured us and scattered us and murdered us; and they kept secret our murder, and did not think of it that they had lifted up their hands against us."

CHAPTER 104

1. I swear to you, just ones, that in heaven the angels will have a remembrance concerning you for good before the glory of the Great One. Your names will be written before the glory of the Great One.

2. Hope, for at first you were disgraced in evil and need, but now you will shine like the luminaries of heaven, and will be seen, and the portals of heaven will be opened to you.

3. And continue your cry for a judgment; it will appear to you, for all your trouble will be avenged on the rulers, and on all those who help those who oppressed you.

4. Hope, and do not cease your hope, for you will have great joy, like the angels in heaven.

5. Since such will be yours, you will not hide on the day of the great judgment, and you will not be found as sinners, and the everlasting judgment will be far from you for all the generations of the world.

6. And now, fear not, you just, when you see the sinners strengthening and rejoicing in their desires, and be not associates with them, but keep far from their oppression, for you will be companions of the hosts of heaven.

7. You sinners, although you say: "You cannot search it out, and all our sins are not written down; still they will continually write down your sins every day.

8. And now I show it to you, that light and darkness, day and night, see all your sins.

9. Be not impious in your hearts, and do not lie, and do not change the words of rectitude, and do not call a lie the words of the Holy and Great One, and do not glorify your idols; for all your untruths and all your impiety will not be to you for a justification, but for a great sin.

10. And now, I know this mystery that the words of rectitude will be changed, and many sinners will rebel, and will speak wicked words, and will lie and make great works, and write books concerning their words.

11. But when they write all my words in righteousness in their languages, and do not change or abridge anything of my words, but write all in rectitude, all that I have first testified on their account,

12. then I know another mystery, that books will be given to just and to the wise for joy and for rectitude and for much wisdom.

13. And the books will be given to them, and they will believe in them and will rejoice in them; and then all the just, who have learned all the paths of rectitude out of them, will be rewarded.

CHAPTER 105

1. "And in those days," says the Lord, "they will call and testify over the sons of the earth concerning their wisdom: show it to them, for you are their leaders, and the rewards over all the earth.

2. For I and my son will join with them to eternity in the paths of rectitude in their lives. And peace will be to you; rejoice, you children of rectitude, in truth!"

CHAPTER 106

1. And after some days, my son Methuselah took a wife for his son Lamech, and she

became pregnant by him, and gave birth to a son.

2. His body was white as snow and red as the bloom of a rose, and the hair of his head was white as wool, and his eyes beautiful; and when he opened his eyes, they illuminated the whole house like the sun, and the whole house became exceedingly light.

3. And as he was taken from the hand of the midwife, he opened his mouth and conversed with the Lord of justice.

4. And his father Lamech was afraid of him, and fled, and came to his father Methuselah.

5. And he said to him: "I have begotten a singular son, unlike a man, but similar to the children of the angels of heaven, and his creation is different, and not like ours, and his eyes are like the feet [i.e. rays] of the sun, his face glorious.

6. And it seems to me he is not from me, but from the angels; and I fear that wonderful thing will happen in his days over the earth.

7. And now, my father, I am here petitioning and asking of you that you should go to Enoch, our father, and hear of

him the truth, for he has his dwelling-place with the angels."

8. And when Methuselah had heard the words of his son, he came to me, at the ends of the earth, for he had heard that I was there, and cried aloud, and I heard his voice and came to him. And I said to him: "Behold, here I am, my son, because you have come to me."

9. And he answered and said to me: "I have come to you concerning a great thing, and concerning a disturbing vision it is that I have approached.

10. And now, my father, hear me, for there has been born to my son Lamech a son, whose similarity and kind is not like the kind of men; his color is whiter than snow and redder than the bloom of a rose, and the hair of his head is whiter than white wool, and his eyes like the feet [i.e. rays] of the sun; and he opened his eyes, and they illuminated the whole house.

11. And when he was taken from the hands of the midwife, he opened his mouth and blessed the Lord of heaven.

12. And his father Lamech was afraid, and fled to me, and

did not believe that he was from him, but that his similarity was from the angels of heaven, and behold I have come to you that you should teach me justice [i.e. the truth]."

13. And I, Enoch, answered, and said to him: "The Lord will make new things on the earth, and this I know and have seen in a vision, and I announce it to you that in the generations of my father Jared some from the heights of heaven departed from the word of the Lord.

14. And behold, they committed sin, and departed from the law, and united themselves with women, and committed sin with them, and married some of them, and begat children from them.

15. And great destruction will be over all the earth, and there will be the water of a deluge, and a great destruction will be for one year.

16. This son who is born to you will be left on the earth, and his three children will be saved with him; when all men who are on the earth will die, he and his children will be saved.

17. [They brought forth on earth giants, not according to the spirit, but according to the flesh, and there will be great punishment on the earth, and the earth will be washed of all of its uncleanness.]

18. And now announce to your son Lamech that he who was born to him is in truth his son, and call his name Noah, for he will be a remnant of you; and he and his children will be saved from the destruction which will come over the earth on account of all the sins and all the injustice which will be completed in his days over the earth.

19. And after that, injustice will exceed that which was first committed on the earth; for I know the mysteries of the holy ones, for he, the Lord, showed me, and has instructed me, and I have read in the tablets of heaven.

CHAPTER 107
1. And I saw written upon them that generation upon generation will transgress till a generation of justice arises, and transgression will be destroyed, and sin will disappear from the earth, and all good will come over it.

2. And now, my son, go and announce to your son Lamech, that this son who is

born is really his, and that this is not a falsehood."

3. And when Methuselah had heard the words of his father Enoch—for he showed him everything that was secret—he returned, after his having seen him, and called the name of that son Noah, for he will make glad the earth for all destruction.

CHAPTER 108

1. Another book that Enoch wrote for his son Methuselah, and for those who come after him, and keep the law in the last days.

2. You who kept it, and now wait in those days till those who did evil are completed, and the power of the transgressors has been completed,

3. wait till sin disappears, for their names will be erased from the books of the holy ones, and their seed will be destroyed to eternity, and their spirits will be killed, and they will cry and lament in a void, empty place, and burn in a fire where there is no end.

4. And there I saw something like a cloud which could not be seen, for from its depths I could not look over it; and I saw a flame of fire burning brightly, and there circled things like shining mountains, and they shook all over.

5. And I asked one of the holy angels who were with me, and said to him; "What is this shining thing? for it is not a heaven, but only the flame of a burning fire, and the voice of shouting and crying and lamenting and of great pain."

6. And he said to me: "This place which you see—here are brought the souls of the sinners and of the revilers and of those who do evil and change everything that God speaks through the mouth of the prophets concerning things to take place.

7. For some of these have been written down, and noted above in heaven, that the angels may read and know what will happen to the sinners and to the spirits of the humble who have chastised their bodies, and for that receive their reward from God, and of those who are reviled by wicked men;

8. Who loved God, and did not love gold or silver or all the riches of the world, but gave over their bodies to torture;

9. And who, since they existed, did not long for terrestrial

112

food, but considered themselves a breath that passes away, and lived accordingly, and were often tried by God, and their spirits were found in cleanness to praise his name.

10. All the blessings they received I have marked down in the books; and he has destined for them their wages, because they have been shown as those who loved the everlasting heaven more than their life, and while they were trodden down by wicked men, and heard abuse and reviling from them, praised me."

11. And now I will call to the spirits of the good, from the generation of light, and change those who were born in darkness, who have not been rewarded in their bodies with honor, as was meet for their fidelity.

12. And I will lead out in a shining light those who love my holy name, and will set each one on the throne of honor, of his honor.

13. And they will glitter in times without number, for justice is the judgment of God, for he will give fidelity to the faithful in the dwellings of the paths of rectitude.

14. And they will see how those who were born in darkness will be cast into darkness, while the just will glitter.

15. And the sinners will cry, and see them as they shine; and they will go there where days and times are written for them.

Suggested Reading

Archie T. Wright, The Origin of Evil Spirits: The Reception of Genesis 6:1-4 in Early Jewish Literature, Revised Edition (Wissenschaftliche Untersuchungen zum Neuen Testament 198, second series; Tübingen: Mohr Siebeck, 2013

Annette Yoshiko Reed, Fallen Angels and the History of Judaism and Christianity: The Reception of Enochic Literature, Cambridge: Cambridge University Press, 2005.

Elizabeth Clare Prophet, Forbidden Mysteries of Enoch: The Untold Story of Men and Angels, Summit University Press, 1983.

George W. E. Nickelsburg and James C. Vanderkam 1 Enoch: A New Translation, Fortress Press, 2004.

George W. E. Nickelsburg, 1 Enoch, v.1: A Commentary on the Book of 1 Enoch, Chapters 1-36, 81-108 Hermeneia: A Critical & Historical Commentary on the Bible, University of Michigan, 2001.

Harkins and Coblentz-Bautch, The Watchers in Jewish and Christian Traditions, Augsberg Fortress Publishers, 2013.

Loren T. Stuckenbruck, 1 Enoch 91-108, Walter de Gruyter, 2008.

Michael S. Heiser, The Unseen Realm: Recovering the Supernatural Worldview of the Bible, Lexham Press, 2015.

Michael S. Heiser, "Are Yahweh and El Distinct Deities in Deut. 32:8-9 and Psalm 82?" HIPHIL 3 (2006); online journal.

Michael S. Heiser, "Deuteronomy 32:8 and the Sons of God," Bibliotheca Sacra 158 (Jan-March, 2001): 52-74

Printed in Poland
by Amazon Fulfillment
Poland Sp. z o.o., Wrocław

12171537R00068